THE
FALSE
FAVORITE

Josh Boldt

First paperback edition January 2020
BlueGood, LLC
Lexington, KY

Cover art by BlueGood Design
www.bluegood.org

ISBN 978-0-578-63258-2

THE
FALSE
FAVORITE

Josh Boldt

1

"You dumb sonofabitch."

The animal snorted and pawed at the ground. Steam shot from its nostrils and swallowed its black head in the cold night air. The barn was dark, but the horse's glassy eyes flashed through the cloud of hot breath. A spotlight mounted on the barn's exterior door dimly lit the inside of the stable. It cast a yellow glow on the face of the horse and the two men who stood before it.

"Just grab him and let's get out of here."

"I can't! He keeps moving!" The man lunged forward, again attempting to toss the bridle over the horse's neck. "What if he kicks me? They do that, you know."

"If you don't quit fooling around I'm gonna kick you myself."

The two men danced uneasily around the giant horse. Each time they made a move forward, the horse countered and blocked their approach.

"Get back behind him in the stall and scare him up here."

"How bout you get back behind him. Here, horsey, we ain't gonna hurt ya. Just come on up here and let us have a look at you."

The man reached slowly forward with the bridle and began to slip it over the long snout. Terror shone in the horse's eyes. Its pupils darted frantically from man to man and around the wooden stall.

"That's it. Easy does it…"

The horse bucked wildly and kicked the back of the stall with a thunderous crash. It reared up on its hind legs and whinnied a warning cry.

"See, he knows we're trying to get him," the man hissed to his partner. "And there ain't no way in hell nobody heard that crash. On a horse farm like this one? We're dead men if we stay here. Come on, we already did the important job. Who gives a damn if this horse don't want to go? Let's just put a bullet in him and get out of here."

"Boss said don't kill the horse. I don't know about you, but I would rather get kicked in the head by this beast than face the boss."

"Yeah, but—"

A light snapped on at another barn about 100 yards across the pasture. The men froze.

"Let's go!"

"What about the horse?"

"Forget the horse. When they find what we left inside the mansion the horse will be the least of our problems. Now go! Run!"

The two men slipped out the back of the barn and ran into the blackness of night.

2

From his seventh-floor office, Cal listened to the city beneath him. The afternoon rain flooded the storm drains on Vine Street. Gutter water whooshed up on the sidewalk with each passing car.

His desk faced the door, and the window behind him was gray. He felt the heavy rain clouds, sensed the sogginess of the city.

A knock at his office door.

He sat up. Rubbed his eyes. Smoothed his hair.

"Yes, come in."

He could see the outline of his visitor through the frosted glass. Shoulders slender and bare. The hall light framed the shape of his guest and cast a yellow slice across the floor of the office to his desk.

The knob turned and the door swung slowly open, spilling light into the room. He squinted his eyes and blinked, adjusting to the change.

Before him stood the silhouette of a woman. The shadows obscured her features. Long, red hair cascaded across her shoulders and down her back.

Her right hand rested on the knob she had just turned. The nails were polished and manicured. She was the first to speak.

"Hiding from someone?" she asked. She squinted through the low dusky light to see Cal seated at his desk across the room. Her voice was low and soft, but confident.

"Aren't you?" he responded and reached over the desk to turn on a lamp.

He twisted the switch and the light snapped on. The area around his desk flooded with soft light, illuminating her features for the first time. She was a beautiful woman. There was no other way to put it, and not a soul in this city would disagree.

She moved across the floor toward Cal's desk with the confidence and grace of a woman who never worried about money.

Cal could see something was wrong. Her eyes were tired, frantic. She hid it well, but the anxiety was there when he looked carefully.

He nodded at the wooden chair in front of his desk. She sat slowly, gripping the edge of her dress and pulling it taut as she lowered herself on to the waiting seat. Knees together, she leaned slightly forward and stared at him across the desk.

"Is there something I can do for you?" he asked.

She looked over his shoulder, through the window and into the darkness of the city but said nothing. Seconds passed. He turned to look in the direction she stared. He knew what he would see. The office building across the street with rooms intermittently lit. Men at desks, pecking at keyboards, opening drawers, scribbling notes, avoiding the inevitable, postponing whatever comes next.

He knew also the gym on the fifth floor. He could see the lap lanes from his office window. Back and forth they swam, splashing toward the wall only to flip, turn, and splash back again. Sometimes he watched the swimmers in the evening, mindlessly observing them cut strokes through the blue-tinted water.

He knew this scene was playing behind him, but he turned to look anyway. More out of an attempt to connect with her than to actually see anything. They sat quietly and watched the swimmers across the dark corridor between the two buildings.

"Do you know who I am?" she finally asked.

He turned his head back toward her with his body still facing the black window. He studied her face. It was familiar, but he couldn't quite place it.

"My husband—" she started. "My ex-hus—I mean my late husband," she finally managed to stammer. "He is well-known. Or, he was well-known," she breathed and then wilted into the darkness.

She receded back to the chair and fumbled in her purse. She withdrew a silver cigarette case and flipped it open with a click. Raising the cigarette to her mouth, she placed it between two red lips and torched the protruding end. Inhale. Exhale. The light from the desk lamp clouded and then slowly the smoke dissipated into the darkness around it.

Her back straightened again and she crossed one leg over the other. The hem of her dress withdrew slightly above her knee. One high heel poked out from the side of the desk. Cal could see the shoe was shiny and black with a red sole.

Returning his gaze to her face, he focused on the glowing cherry of the cigarette. She raised it again to her lips and its fiery tip flamed bright in response to her fresh draw of oxygen.

"Who is—was—your husband?" Cal asked.

"I hope you don't mind if I smoke," she exhaled and squinted her green eyes to avoid the smoke that wafted from the burning cigarette.

Cal shrugged in response.

"What do you know about the Kentucky Derby?" she asked pointedly, almost accusingly.

He had lived in Kentucky long enough to know what the Derby meant to the state. Both Louisville and Lexington shut down on Derby Day, and the people of these cities are devoted to the sport of horse racing. You don't desecrate the hallowed event to a Kentuckian, no matter what your personal opinion is of the holiday.

"I have been known to visit the track for a mint julep or two," he responded.

Her eyes narrowed and she smiled slightly.

"Then you have probably heard of my husband. Sterling Leighton Halcott." She drew again from the cigarette and re-crossed her legs.

He turned fully around to face her now with his eyes opened wide. He rarely betrayed surprise to a client, but this time he couldn't suppress his incredulity.

"Wait a minute. You're telling me you are Harper Halcott?"

"Yes."

"Of the Halcott family, who owns practically every thoroughbred in this state?"

"Yes."

"Your husband? He's, he's rich."

"Was," she replied, and lowered her eyes to the desktop.

She paused for a second before spotting a thick glass ashtray. She reached for the amber glass and stubbed out the cigarette. A strand of red hair slid off her shoulder and dropped like a pendulum between them, resting on the front edge of the desk.

She quickly leaned back in her seat and waited for Cal's response.

Of course he had heard the news. It was all over the wire. Millionaire playboy and horse racing darling Sterling Leighton Halcott had died suddenly last week in what the media was reporting to be a suicide. The metro police had called it an open and shut investigation. Suicide note and a bullet in the head. Case closed.

According to reports, Halcott had intimated in the suicide note he believed his life had peaked and he could see nowhere to go but down. He was exhausted with his jet-setting lifestyle and worried public interest in the horse racing industry was waning. His empire was on the verge of collapse and he could not bear to watch it happen. He had chosen to quit while he was on top.

A press leak from the autopsy report indicated Halcott's blood contained high levels of alcohol and cocaine, and the authorities believed he had simply acted impulsively early one morning after coming down from a bender.

"I'm sorry," he said. "He seemed to have everything."

"He did. And that was his biggest problem," she responded and then she was quiet again.

"How are you dealing with this tragedy?" he asked after a few seconds of silence.

Without waiting for her to respond, he stood and walked over to the cabinet against the wall. He swung open the door and produced two glasses and a half-empty bottle of Wild Turkey. He lifted the bottle and showed it to her inquisitively. She nodded. He popped the cork and poured a shot of the brown liquid into both glasses.

Taking a drink in each hand, he turned toward her. He handed her one of the lowballs and leaned against the front edge of his desk, still palming his own glass of bourbon.

She took the drink and raised it to her lips. Her eyes closed as she swallowed the liquor. When she opened her eyes, they shone brighter and appeared to be slightly damp. Cal couldn't tell if this effect was produced by tears or the burn of the alcohol.

She reached forward and set the empty glass on the lip of the desk. He noticed her faint perfume for the first time as she reached past him. It was familiar, nostalgic somehow. Lavender mixed with a spice…maybe clove or cinnamon?

She tilted her head toward him, and her eyes were again clear. Ignoring his question, she instead asked one of her own to no one in particular.

"Why would he do this now? One month away from the Derby? It just doesn't make any sense. He loved the Derby. It was his favorite time of year."

Cal could tell she didn't believe the police reports. And, frankly, he didn't either. Something was not matching up. Something appeared to be off with the whole story. He had been keeping an eye on it himself for the past week, scouring the press reports for clues, for some indication of foul play. So far, he had come up with nothing but questions.

Of course, he had no idea one week after Halcott's death, the widow would be seated in his office sharing those same suspicions.

"I'm glad you are here, but I have to ask. Why? Why did you knock on my door tonight?"

3

"I can't trust anyone. The chief of police came to all of our parties. Not even a month ago, he was smoking cigars on the veranda with my husband and all of his friends."

"Why is that a problem?" Cal asked.

"I'm afraid the chief is in their pockets. I have seen so many hundred-dollar handshakes I have lost count. If one of my husband's friends is involved in his death, I have no doubt palms have been greased enough to make the whole thing disappear."

He nodded slightly and took a sip from the glass of bourbon. He stood and walked slowly back around to his chair on the other side of the desk. As he sat, he slid open the drawer to his right and retrieved a notepad and pen.

- *Trust no one*
- *Possible inside job*

He looked up from his notes and fixed his eyes back on Harper, waiting for her to continue the story.

"I can't go to the metro police. They have already closed the book on my husband's death. As far as I can tell, they don't plan to investigate a single detail. When I called the detective he treated me like a child. I need to get some rest, he said. I should talk to a psychiatrist. Try not to get too excited. The more paranoid I get, the more patronizing he becomes."

Cal listened intently. He had dealt with the metro police on numerous occasions and had occasionally run into the same wall Harper was now hitting. He had heard rumors of corruption, the implications of horse money influencers. Some even argue the thoroughbred industry controls the local economy, and not a decision is made in this state without input from the few golden families who own eighty percent of the land in the Bluegrass region.

"I have nowhere else to turn. I need someone on the outside who can look in and dig up the dirt I believe is being swept under the rug. My husband had many friends, and he also had many enemies. I believe one of them is responsible for his death, and I need to find out who. Can you help me? Will you help me?"

Her eyes glistened again. She was remarkably composed for a woman whose husband had just committed suicide one week before. But if she was hiding something, she was doing a good job of it. She seemed earnest. She wanted his help. And besides, he was personally interested in the case. He had to take it.

"My usual fee is $200 a day, plus expenses. But this case is unusual. It's dangerous and it will require some risky work."

14

"Money is of no concern to me. I have more than I could ever spend. Will $1,000 a day suffice?" she asked, reaching into her bag and removing a leather pocketbook. "Use this to get started and bill me for the rest."

She spoke into the checkbook as she scrawled out her signature. Her nails wagged back and forth as the pen made long strokes on the check. Perfectly manicured. The lamp's bulb reflected in the deep red paint.

The ripping of the check broke Cal's trance, tearing through the silence. She slid the check across the desk and rose from her chair.

"Do you have everything you need to get started?"

"Yes, I believe so. Just one more question. Who would you say was your husband's biggest enemy?"

She thought for a moment, staring again out the window at the lights of the city.

"Three possibilities come to mind," she finally replied. "Augusto Gallo, the Argentine breeder who sends horses up to run in all of the major Kentucky meets. He and my husband used to meet in Miami a few times each year to discuss business and thoroughbreds. They acted friendly, but they were in deep competition and I am sure either would have loved to see the other disappear."

"Second is our former trainer, Jubal Early. We let him go in January. My husband wanted to start this season fresh with a new trainer. He felt Jubal wasn't doing what was necessary to bring home the roses this year, and he decided to let him go. Since January, we have seen Early wandering around the stables a few times and we eventually had to ask John Hood, our head of security, to bar him from the grounds. According to John, Early became agitated and had to be forcibly removed from the barn where our prized horses are housed."

Cal jotted down a few more notes on his pad as he listened.

- *Investigate former trainer*
- *Pull criminal record and work history*

She continued, "And third would be practically anyone from PETA. We constantly face scrutiny from the organization due to our involvement in the horse racing industry. Let's just say they don't like us much."

"Interesting. Makes sense, I guess," he replied. "Well, Ms. Halcott, this should do for now. I have a good start here. I will let you know as soon as I find anything."

"Thank you. And please call me Harper."

She picked up her bag and turned to go.

"Wait, one more thing," he called after her.

She looked back over her shoulder.

"Yes?"

"I'll need access to the Derby parties you and your husband would normally attend over the course of the next month."

He knew Louisville was more or less one big party between now and the first Saturday in May. The week before Derby the debauchery would rise to a crescendo and any celebrity who was anybody could be found at the mansions within a 20-mile radius of Churchill Downs. If there was information to be gleaned, it could be overheard in the conversations at one of those elaborate soirees.

"Of course. I will make sure you are on all the lists."

"Thank you, Ms.—I mean Harper. Good night."

"Good night, Mr. Tyson."

She tilted her head slightly and smiled before vanishing out his door into the yellow hall light.

He sat quietly at his desk, staring into the space she had just vacated. This was going to be a dangerous case. People with this kind of money can do anything they want. They can make people vanish into thin air and then close the book before anyone asks questions. The families he would be investigating were some of the richest and most powerful people in the country.

Harper's check lay on the desk by his notepad. He turned it over. A one followed by five zeros.

"That'll do," he thought to himself. "At least it's one good thing about the trouble I am getting myself into."

He stood and walked to the window. The gym across the street was dark now. The swimmers had all gone home. Most of the offices were also dark. The keyboards were silent, the papers were filed, the drawers were closed for the day.

Cal sipped the glass of bourbon and watched the city below as it transitioned to night.

4

The rain stopped overnight, leaving the city washed and wet. From the window table, Cal could see the intersection of Upper and Short. Clay's Diner occupied the ground floor of a historic apartment building across from the old courthouse, directly in the center of the city. Lawyers and stockbrokers with briefcases. The morning slid by.

A white porcelain mug rested carefully on the table to Cal's right with a napkin over it. He liked knowing how much coffee he drank. He never wanted to be topped off.

The grease of a thousand hogs hung thickly in the air. The kind of place where your clothes remember what you ate for breakfast long into the afternoon. Bacon sizzled in the short order kitchen and the sweet smell of melting butter balanced the acidic overtone of hotplate coffee.

"Two eggs with sausage and toast." The waitress placed the plate in front of Cal and sauntered back to the kitchen.

He lifted the top piece of toast to check it had been buttered. It had, but it was cold. Why do they do that, he wondered. The toast should be the last item cooked. Rather cold eggs than cold toast.

At the street corner across from him, a woman was clasping the tiny paw of a child in each hand. They crossed Short Street walking towards Main. As they neared his window, Cal spotted a canvas tote slung over her shoulder. "Friends of the Library" it declared in big red letters.

One of the boys had climbed on to the rock wall surrounding the old courthouse, causing his mother to raise her right arm. The three strolled along the sidewalk each taller than the next. She carefully grasped the hand of each child, arms askew like a scarecrow.

"You alright there, bud?"

Cal snapped back to reality. A bite of over-medium egg slid off the end of his fork and slapped back to the porcelain plate. Looking up, he spotted the gray-bearded Ed Masters, his inside contact at the Lexington *Herald-Leader*.

"Hm? Oh, just thinking about something."

"Well, don't think too hard before 8:00 a.m. That's what I always say. How you been, buddy? Long time, no see."

Ed slumped into the seat across from Cal. He was a longtime newspaperman and there wasn't a soul on the planet who could go toe-to-toe with Ed on the topic of thoroughbred history. He had a hand in every article the *Herald-Leader* published on the subject, and he was a staple at both Keeneland and the Red Mile, two local Lexington racetracks.

"I've got a real doozy for you today, Ed. You aren't going to believe who was in my office last night."

Ed motioned in the direction of the waitress and raised his hand as though lifting an imaginary coffee cup to his mouth. She got the drift and disappeared into the kitchen to retrieve the pot of black coffee.

"I just love this place, don't you?" Ed asked. "It's right in the middle of town, but it doesn't get near enough credit."

Cal nodded in agreement, thinking about his cold toast.

"Well, what's the big secret?" Ed prodded. "Let me guess, you're getting yourself into trouble with this Halcott mess?"

"You know me too well," Cal replied. "Harper Halcott herself smoked a cigarette in my office last night."

"No shit? I've only ever seen her on TV. She as hot as she looks?"

Cal ignored the question and proceeded with the story. "She doesn't believe the police reports. Thinks the whole story is fishy and asked me to look into it."

"She's not the only one. You should have heard the response from the newsroom when word came down we were reporting it as a routine suicide. The place was an uproar. My editor straight-faced the whole deal and then closed his office door for the rest of the day. It was a goddamn joke."

It was Cal's turn to be surprised. How could everyone see so plainly there was more to this story, but yet give in so easily?

The waitress appeared at the edge of the table with a pot of steaming hot coffee and a white ceramic mug, which she turned over and placed on a saucer in front of Ed.

"How you this morning, honey?" she asked, flashing Ed a smile.

He raised his eyes and smiled back. "I'll be a hell of a lot better after I get one of those tasty Denver omelets in my stomach."

It was clear they knew each other. She nodded assent and returned to her post at the counter to ring in his order. Ed watched her move away from the table, more because he was looking in that direction than for any other reason.

"Listen, Ed, I could really use some assistance on this one. Harper is connecting me to all of the big Derby parties in Louisville and I need your help coming up with the key players I should be watching for. You know every person in the industry and whether or not they matter. Can you help me come up with a list?"

"Harper, eh? You guys are already on a first name basis I see," Ed teased. "Of course, pal, you know I'm good for it. Just keep me in the loop on any new information you uncover . . ." He trailed off and winked.

Cal stood up and extended his hand for Ed to shake. "Good to see you again, my friend. Enjoy your breakfast."

"You know I will. I'll shoot an email over to you later this afternoon with some names." He shook hands, nodded in valediction, and returned to his coffee. Cal heard Ed's mug clink in its saucer as he pushed the diner door open and stepped into the morning rush of Short Street.

5

The Main Street branch of the Public Library has become little more than a homeless shelter, Cal thought as he climbed the winding staircase to the second floor. He stepped on the landing and surveyed the atrium. Every chair was full of bums who were either sleeping, talking loudly, or staring blankly into space. He walked over to the huge floor-to-ceiling windows that overlooked Phoenix Park below.

Traffic was at a standstill on Limestone. One of its lanes had been closed for over a year due to construction on the Middle Mark high rise. A year ago, a gaping hole was dug right into the center of the city in preparation for this project. Nothing had been done since. The massive excavation site now sat untouched in the center of downtown, bordered first by chain link and then by closed road lanes, like the scab of a giant metastasizing scar.

He turned away from the window in the direction of the elevators.

"Fourth floor: Periodicals," the elevator chimed. He stepped out and headed for the help desk where a bespectacled librarian was seated, awaiting his request for assistance.

Cal approached the desk and leaned over it. "How far back do you keep newspaper copies?" he asked.

She looked up from her book, sliding an index card between the pages to mark her spot. Cal recognized the peacock feather on the cover. *The Collected Short Stories of Flannery O'Connor.*

She lifted her glasses from the bridge of her nose and let them drop to her chest. A colorful chain was attached to each hinge of the glasses. It reached just far enough to rest the lenses on the neck of her cardigan, an inch below the first open button on her dotted blouse.

"We keep several local papers on file. Which are you interested in?" Her voice was soft, soothing, warm.

"The *Herald-Leader* and the *Courier-Journal,* for starters. And do you keep issues of *BloodHorse?*"

"We keep one month of back issues in print for the *Herald-Leader* and *Courier-Journal.* We don't get many requests for *BloodHorse.* It's pretty industry specific. Are you a breeder?"

"No, just a fan of the sport."

"Okay. Follow me and I will take you to the newspaper archives. As for the horse racing news, we do have some periodicals and journals I can show you, but I also recommend you check online." She stepped from behind the help desk and headed toward the stacks.

He followed her yellow skirt as she cut across the marble floor and squeezed between carts piled high with books. Rows of computers with dancing screensavers. Note pads and boxes full of tiny golf pencils. She stopped in front of a door marked ARCHIVES.

"You should be able to find everything you need in here. Let me know if I can be of any more assistance," she said as she swung the door open and switched on the light. Cal smiled and squeezed past her into the quiet room.

The stale smell of ink and yellowed paper burned his nostrils as he inhaled and suppressed a slight cough. He heard the librarian chuckle as she pulled the door closed behind him.

The room was lined with shelves and boxes. Each box was marked with the name of the publication it contained.

New York Times, Wall Street Journal, Washington Post, L. A. Times

Finally, his eyes rested on a red-lettered sign with the word LOCAL stenciled on it. It hung above a shelf full of boxes with newspapers he recognized. He reached for the *Herald-Leader* and *Courier-Journal* boxes and pulled them off the shelf, placing them on a large wooden table in the center of the room.

He wasn't exactly sure what he was looking for. Just hoping something would jump out at him. Any article related to horse racing or the Kentucky gentry, he set to the side. The Keeneland spring meet had just opened in Lexington, so the *Herald-Leader* was packed with stories about thoroughbreds and wagering tips for novice bettors.

Announcements for upcoming Derby parties and social events littered the pages of the *Courier-Journal*. Derby season was in full swing.

Then he spotted it. The March 25th issue of the *Courier-Journal* had a full-page article on Halcott Farms and its Derby hopefuls. Smack in the center of the page was a photograph of Sterling and Harper Halcott flanking a powerful-looking horse. Around the couple were several of their closest friends and industry insiders. The caption read:

Halcott Farms looks for a Derby repeat this year with the fast and pedigreed Valkyrie. Pictured from left: Sterling Halcott, owner; Harper Halcott, owner; Jubal Early, trainer."

That's odd, Cal thought to himself. I thought the Halcotts fired Early in January. Why would he be featured prominently in this photo from March with his name listed as the primary trainer for Valkyrie?

He pulled the notepad from his shirt pocket and flipped it open to his most recent note. Sure enough, Harper had told him Early was let go in January.

- Ask Harper about photo

His notes reminded him of the plan to investigate Early in more detail. He snapped a picture of the *Courier-Journal* photo and took a seat in front of the only computer in the Archives room.

He slid the mouse on its felt pad and the black screen came to life.

"Jubal Early," he typed into the search bar. The page lit up with results, but they weren't about the Jubal Early he thought he was investigating.

"What the?" he asked aloud. "Jubal Early, Civil War Lt. General of the Confederate States of America. Born November 3, 1816. Died March 2, 1894 in Lynchburg, Va. There's no way this is a coincidence. It's such an unusual name. Could he be related to the Halcotts' former trainer?"

He clicked the Wikipedia entry for the deceased Civil War general.

Jubal Anderson Early was a lawyer and Confederate general in the American Civil War. He served under Stonewall Jackson and then Robert E. Lee for almost the entire war, rising from regimental command to lieutenant general and the command of an infantry corps in the Army of Northern Virginia. He was the Confederate commander in key battles of the Valley Campaigns of 1864, including a daring raid to the outskirts of Washington, D.C. The articles written by him for the Southern Historical Society in the 1870s established the Lost Cause point of view as a long-lasting literary and cultural phenomenon.

"Lost Cause?" Cal asked the empty room and clicked the hyperlink.

The Lost Cause is a regional American cultural movement, based in the white South, seeking to reconcile the traditionalist white society of the antebellum South that they admire, to the defeat of the Confederate States of America in the American Civil War of 1861–1865. Supporters typically portray the Confederacy's cause as noble and most of its leaders as exemplars of old-fashioned chivalry, defeated by the Union armies through numerical and industrial force that overwhelmed the South's superior military skill and courage.

"I'll be darned. You learn something new every day." Cal was still talking to himself. "Well, just because Early might have descended from this character doesn't mean he ascribes to any of his beliefs. I'll have to set up an interview with him. I need to figure out a way to get him to talk without revealing I'm investigating the case."

Cal was so engrossed in his research he had not heard the Archives room door open at his back or the footsteps on the soft carpet.

"Investigating what case?"

Cal nearly jumped out of his skin when he heard the voice behind him. He turned to see the librarian in the doorway. She was laughing at his startled reaction.

"I'm sorry," she laughed. " I thought you heard me come in."

He exhaled deeply and shook his head. How long had she been listening?

"You aren't just a fan of the thoroughbred industry, are you? What kind of investigation are you conducting on the Old South?"

"Oh, it's nothing," he stammered, attempting to regain his composure. "Just doing some research."

She saw right through him. "Well, you happen to be in luck. I wrote my master's thesis on antebellum history and I have an entire chapter about the Southern Historical Society. Maybe I can help."

She closed the door behind her and crossed the room, pausing to study the newspapers spread out on the table. She pulled a chair up to the desk and looked him in the eye.

"Who are you really? What exactly is going on here?"

6

Cal blinked. He knew he was caught. Should he make up a story? She might actually be able to help him. Maybe he should tell the truth and enlist her services. He was clearly out of his element on the history piece of this investigation, and she might be a valuable resource. Besides, she wasn't exactly hard on the eyes…

He exhaled and turned his chair to face her. She sensed the importance of what he was about to say and leaned in, narrowing her eyes as if to block out all other distractions while she listened.

"Have you heard about the Halcott suicide?"

"Um, of course. Who hasn't? Please tell me you are some kind of private investigator who is researching the case," she replied, half-joking.

"I'm some kind of private investigator who is researching the case."

"No way. You have to be kidding. We have a private investigator in Lexington, Kentucky? What are you trying to find out?"

"Well, for starters, I don't believe Halcott committed suicide. And neither does his widow."

"Wait. You think he was…murdered?" she trailed off as she spoke the final word.

"I do. And you overheard me talking about one of the prime suspects. His name is Jubal Early, and he is the estranged head trainer at Halcott Farms."

"Jubal Early like the Civil War general?"

"The very one."

"Weird. Do you think he's a descendant?"

"Possibly. I'm curious to find that out, among other things."

"Okay, so he's the one you want to schedule a meeting with I guess. How do you plan to get close enough to him without blowing your cover?"

"Haven't gotten that far yet. Any ideas?" he asked, smiling.

"Yeah, you could take me along to pose as your wife who's interested in hiring a new trainer for our imaginary horse farm. Sounds to me like he is out of a job and might be looking to meet a wealthy couple with thoroughbreds."

"Oh, you're good. I think I like you," Cal replied.

She smiled and averted her gaze, a bit embarrassed by her own forwardness and the intimacy implied in her creative scenario. She raised her eyes back to meet his. Her embarrassment was gone in an instant and she returned to her confident composure.

"Good. Let's do this. By the way, I'm Emma."

That's a first, Cal thought to himself as he pushed open the library's heavy double doors and stepped out on the pavement of Phoenix Park.

"I really hope I didn't make a mistake," he spoke under his breath. But there was something about Emma that reassured him of the decision. And besides, what a great idea for pulling one over on Early.

He shook off his inhibition and rounded the corner on Vine Street, heading east back to his office.

Waiting in his inbox was an email from Ed Masters containing a list of about 30 names he should watch for at the Derby parties in Louisville.

Keep a close eye on these high rollers. If anyone knows something about Halcott, it's almost certainly one of them. And be sure to slip me a lead if you find one!

Cal recognized many of the names on the list. Thoroughbred owners, trainers, even a couple of jockeys. A few politicians and local personalities also made it on Ed's watchlist.

Valuable information. Cal printed the list, folded it, and placed it in his back pocket.

"Let's see here, Jubal. How do you feel about taking on some new work?" he mumbled as he dialed the phone number he had found for Early.

Ring.

Ring.

Ring.

"Jubal Early here," the voice on the other end of the line spoke.

"Yes. Hi, Mr. Early. I understand you are the man to talk to when it comes to producing Derby winners." A little flattery never hurt.

Early was guarded, suspicious. "Maybe so. Who's asking?"

"My name is Cap Barclay and I own a horse farm outside of Bowling Green. My wife and I are looking to break into the thoroughbred industry—we currently have a few horses—and we are seeking a reputable trainer who can take us to the next level."

"Never heard of you," was the gruff response.

"Well, we aren't particularly well-known just yet, but we hope to be soon with your help. We will miss the Derby this year, of course, but we have our eyes on the rose garland next year."

This seemed to loosen Early up a bit. "Yeah, ok. Well, I've taken two horses to the Winner's Circle already and I can do it again."

"Excellent. Can we set up a time to discuss a possible arrangement? Are you in Louisville?"

"Jeffersonville. Across the river. How about Monday at 10:00 a.m.? There's a little diner on Riverside Drive where I eat breakfast. Right off I-65."

"It's a deal. My wife and I look forward to meeting you, Mr. Early."

"Yeah, ok," he replied and hung up.

Cal returned the phone to the receiver and smiled at how easy it was to arrange the meeting.

"Emma, I like you more every minute," he said and laughed at his good fortune.

But arranging the meeting is the easy part. Now they have to get him to talk.

7

Cool leather of the office couch. Afternoon sunlight streaming in from the window behind his desk. Footsteps in the hallway. Cal glanced around the room, checking to make sure everything was how he left it. His eyes rested on the window and its warm light.

Even after a nap, bacon grease from the diner was still faintly detectable on his wrinkled shirt. It smelled good against the backdrop of worn leather. Like breakfast hash at an Irish pub.

He guessed it was about four o'clock. He felt for the cell phone he knew was somewhere on the floor below him. His fingers touched the cold metal and he raised the phone to his chest, still lying on the couch.

Opening the text messages, he typed the phone number Emma had given him earlier.

Hey, we're good on Jubal. Can you take Monday off?

He tossed the phone on the couch and sat up. It's Friday afternoon. Maybe I'll grab a drink.

His phone buzzed on the cushion next to him.

I knew that would get him. Yep, Monday is clear. So, what's the plan?

He spoke aloud to himself, laughing at the ridiculousness of the situation. "I guess we should get to know each other considering we're supposed to be married."

How do you feel about grabbing a drink this evening? Shortside around 7?

I feel pretty good about it. See you then!

Cal couldn't help smiling. "Remember this is business," he said and shook his head as if to dispel a thought that was creeping into his consciousness.

He stood up and stretched, then walked over to the window and looked out at the bright blue sky. Shadows of afternoon had begun to stretch long the objects on his desk. Not a bad day so far, he thought. Of course, that can always change.

The fountain at Thoroughbred Park was full of splashing children. Although Shortside was just a quick walk from his office, he had time to kill, so he took the long way around downtown. It was a pretty afternoon and he wanted to grab a coffee on Eastern Avenue.

Cal strolled past the fountain and across the street. As usual, the door was propped open at the coffee shop.

Just for fun, he scanned the Pay it Forward board where people can buy coffees in advance for their friends and hang a note on the wall to be claimed later. His name had never appeared on the wall, but he liked to study it anyway and read the handwritten notes.

"The usual, Cal?" spoke a voice behind him. It was the closest coffee shop to his office, so he was a regular. His usual was a coffee, black.

He turned to face the voice. "Please," he replied, nodding.

Coffee in hand, he returned to Thoroughbred Park and found a seat on a metal bench near the fountain. He sensed the heightened awareness of the parents whose children were splashing a few feet away. It's a shame the creeps and weirdos have ruined a single man's ability to simply enjoy the sight of happy kids, he thought to himself. Now everyone thinks a man is a pederast if he sits on a park bench alone.

He sipped the coffee. It doesn't matter how hot it gets outside. Cal could always drink a cup of steaming joe.

From his seat, he could see past the fountain to the park's namesake. Seven life-sized metal horses frozen in time, in a never-ending race. The front horse will always lead and those behind it will always follow until the day this park is demolished.

No matter the time of day at Thoroughbred Park, someone is always posing for a photograph with those perpetually-racing horses.

Cal lounged on the park bench, taking in the afternoon, sipping coffee, and watching people enjoy themselves. The Herald-Leader building stood in the distance beyond the metal horses. He wondered if Ed was still in the office at this hour. With Keeneland open, he guessed Ed had taken the afternoon off and headed straight for the track. He knew from experience the first post was 1:15 on Fridays.

Last sip. Cal tossed the empty cup into the recycling can about ten feet away. Three kids cheered and applauded from the fountain. He stood, smiled, and bowed elaborately.

Shortside is a twenty-minute walk and it's only 6:00. Oh well, he would be a little early. He turned west on Main and faced the city before him.

8

Blues guitar sliced through the open front door of Shortside as Cal neared the bar. The bluesman's Fender was plugged into an amplifier on the stage next to him. He played without accompaniment. The sound was just loud enough to entertain the happy hour patrons and draw in passersby from the pavilion outside. Not too loud that you couldn't sit at the bar and have a conversation.

Cal approached the long, wooden bar and slid on to a stool, placing his elbows atop the shiny lacquer.

"Bourbon and ginger," he spoke to the youngish bartender leaning against the liquor rack behind the bar. The bartender reached across his body with his right hand and slid a white towel off his left shoulder. He wiped his hands clean and tucked the towel into the back of his waistband.

"Bourbon preference?"

"Woodford."

Behind Cal, the bluesman moaned.

> *Baby, please don't go. Now, baby, please don't go.*
> *Baby, please don't go back to New Or-leans*
> *Because I love you so. Baby, please don't go.*

As he sang, he stared straight ahead in a trance. Over the tables, over the bar, over the servers who were milling around the open dining room. Straight through the wall and the patio, across Mill Street, across Broadway, across west Lexington and all the way to I-64.

Cal watched the bartender count as he tilted the bottle of Woodford Reserve toward the waiting highball glass. One . . . Two. Stop. The jigger closed and the amber ceased flowing. Two ice cubes. Top it with a splash of ginger ale. Stirring straw. Black napkin.

Cal guessed the guy to be about 25. Maybe a recent Transylvania University grad or a new UK law student. Both schools were within an easy walk from the restaurant.

He rested his fingertips on the edge of the bar napkin and dragged the whole package toward him. With his other hand he lifted the glass as he held down the napkin to keep it from sticking.

Sitting back casually, drink in hand, Cal surveyed the bar.

The stage was positioned at the front of the large room and raised a step above the dining area it faced. Behind it were windows overlooking an outdoor pavilion, a local gathering spot in the center of downtown where the people of Lexington congregate at happy hour to unwind and sip cocktails under a covered patio.

He glanced at his watch. A notch before seven. The skyline, which Cal could see over the shaking shoulders of the wailing bluesman, was just beginning to turn pink.

The bar where Cal sat ran the length of one side of the room. The other side was flanked by a row of cozy booths. In the middle were a few sparsely placed tables. A lawyer jotting notes on a brief, a loner staring into space, first daters nervously pecking at their plates. Furtive glances. A group of graduate students feverishly debating at the booth nearest Cal. He leaned in slightly and listened.

"Everything we consider to be modern philosophy descended from Derrida," one of the grad students was saying. "Without *Of Grammatology*, there would be no postmodernism. There would be no *Simpsons* or any of the metahumor-based television that followed it. There would be—"

"What are you talking about!" interrupted a second man. "There wouldn't even be any Derrida without Ferdinand de Saussure and Heidegger. And neither of them without Plato!"

"Are you saying Plato was the original Deconstructionist?" the woman in the group asked.

Nervous laughter.

"All of those dudes can kiss my ass. Literary theory is a waste of time," said a third guy with a sleeve tattoo and a pair of thick, black-rimmed glasses. "Don't you guys know the critic is dead?"

Emma climbed up on the bar stool next to Cal and nodded sideways toward the grad students, who were now practically shouting at each other about the relevance of Roland Barthes.

"Wow, that's one heck of a happy hour conversation," she said.

"Yeah, somebody better cut them off," Cal smiled as he rotated his bar stool back toward the front of the room to face Emma.

"So how was your day, husband?" Her tone was one of nervous excitement. She knew it was a bit daring to immediately pick up the role she had chosen for herself earlier that day, but she did it anyway.

Cal couldn't deny a slight thrill at the implication, but he responded coolly.

"Jubal was a piece of cake. He never saw us coming. I think we should be able to get a good read on him after our meeting Monday morning."

"*We*, eh? You're assuming I want to be part of this affair after our one-time ruse?" She smiled and stared him down, waiting for an answer.

"Well, don't you?" he fired back.

"Yep."

Her confidence made Cal a little shy. Had he just asked for a second date?

"Good. Do you know anything about the city of Louisville?"

"You mean other than the fact I grew up in the Highlands and went to high school at Sacred Heart?"

"Oh god. Isn't that a Catholic School?"

"Oh god is right. I couldn't escape that place fast enough. But the point is, yeah, I know Louisville."

She lifted her hand to flag the bartender and ordered a Johnny Walker neat.

Cal raised his eyebrows slightly but said nothing.

"So I've known you all of eight hours and you have already made me your wife and your tour guide. Watch out for this guy." She spoke the last sentence facetiously, raising her scotch in a mock toast to the rack of liquor bottles behind the bar.

Cal watched their reflection in the mirror behind the bar as she sipped her drink and returned it to the bar top. The April sky was coloring over the bluesman's shoulder. Cal turned to face her. He looked into her eyes and spoke.

"Have you ever been to a Derby party?"

9

Friday night and the city had come to life by the time Cal crossed Limestone on his way home from Shortside. Limestone is the main corridor into downtown from the University of Kentucky's campus. On Friday night, throngs of college students pour out of dorms and stumble three blocks to one of the local hangouts known for serving copious amounts of booze.

Cal made a right on Limestone and headed toward campus. Two frat guys were supporting a third kid whose legs had stopped communicating with his brain. As they stumbled past, Cal heard the wobbly one mumble something about an Irish Car Bomb. Clearly what this kid needs is another drink. In their wake they left scattered beer cans and a cacophony of cheap cologne and Axe body spray.

Cal was a bit drunk himself. Turns out Emma was pretty fun to talk to, and they had a few more drinks at Shortside before calling it a night.

"What are the chances she would be from Louisville?" He spoke the question quietly to himself. Dumb luck how all of these pieces seem to be falling into place.

"Almost perfect. Maybe too perfect?"

He was still talking to himself as he turned left on Maxwell heading in the direction of home.

Suddenly he became conscious of the faint sound of footsteps about twenty paces behind him. He snapped out of his daydream and listened carefully as he walked.

Yes, he definitely heard footsteps. They were on the other side of Maxwell and maybe half a block back.

Should I turn to look? Not yet. If you're being followed, don't let on you know.

He walked on in silence for two more blocks, listening carefully. At Woodland Avenue he made a sudden right and increased his pace a little. As he turned, he glanced back over his shoulder.

Sure enough, a man in a dark grey suit and hat was half a block behind him, matching his pace. Entirely possible this guy works downtown and is walking home just like I am, Cal thought. But let's play it safe. He ducked into McIntyre's at the corner of Woodland and Euclid for a nightcap.

McIntyre's is the type of place old men go to make the world disappear. It's a depressing, down and out joint that used to be a cool hangout in the 90s, but now rarely hosts more than a handful of sad sacks who sit dejectedly at the bar and stare into their pint glasses.

Cal ordered a beer and grabbed a booth in the back corner so he could keep an eye on the door. The floor under him stuck to his shoes and the stench in the bar was rancid. Like a 70-year-old alcoholic's vomit breath.

As Cal settled in, one of the old drunks at the bar started to get belligerent.

"You see this tattoo?" the drunk slurred to anyone who would listen. He raised his right shirt sleeve to his elbow, exposing the ink. No one in the bar so much as lifted their head in acknowledgement.

The drunk continued. "You know what my old man said when he saw this tattoo? He said 'you look like a pussy!'"

The guy was practically shouting to the open room now. Still no one even bothered to turn around.

"He said 'you look like a little pussy with that tattoo!' God love that bastard. He was an asshole. I hope he's burning in hell."

The drunk's maniacal laughter rang through the barroom. It quickly turned to a hacking cough and then silence again as though nothing had ever happened.

A waitress was sweeping crumbs from under one of the tables. The bartender shifted his weight to the other leg and stared blankly at a television mounted in the corner.

...questions swirling around Halcott Farms in the wake of millionaire playboy Sterling Halcott's suicide...Derby officials wondering if favorite Valkyrie will still be at the post on May 7th...widow Harper Halcott denies rumors the horse will be pulled from this year's contest...

The door swung open and the man in the grey suit entered the bar. Cal froze in his seat. The grey fedora shadowed the man's eyes, but Cal could see from his reaction they hadn't yet adjusted to the tavern's dim lighting.

The shouting drunk turned to examine the newcomer. He sniffed loudly and then promptly dropped his forehead on the bar.

The newcomer glanced about the room and approached the bar. He ordered a drink quietly. Cal couldn't hear what he was saying, but he saw the bartender lean in to listen.

After a few seconds, the bartender shook his head and shrugged. "I don't know anything about it."

The grey-suited man was visibly perturbed by this response. He stood up and tipped his shot glass back, tossing the liquor down his throat. He fumbled in his pocket for a crumpled bill, threw it on the bar, and disappeared out the door as quickly as he had come in.

Cal swallowed the last of his beer and stepped up to the bar in exactly the place the grey-suited man had just stood.

"Hey, what was that about?" he asked the bartender.

"I don't know, man. That guy was weird."

"In what way?"

"Why do you care?"

Cal slid a $20 across the bar and withdrew his hand.

"I just do. What did he ask you about?"

The bartender looked at Cal quizzically and palmed the twenty.

"He asked if I knew where to find a titty bar. Hell, I don't mess with those joints. Waste of money if you ask me."

Cal relaxed and leaned back from the bar. False alarm.

The bartender was still talking.

"But I guess if you have an eye like that dude does, you probably have to pay somebody to fuck you."

That got Cal's attention again. "Why, what was wrong with his eye?"

"His left eye was sliced all to hell. It looked like he lost a knife fight. Or maybe he won, I don't know. Anyway, aside from the scar, his whole eyeball was white. I've never seen anything like it. Pretty nasty shit."

Cal winced at the description. Probably nothing, but he should be more careful.

He thanked the bartender for the intel and followed the path of the one-eyed man into the black night.

10

Morning.

Sky over Woodford County bright blue without a cloud in sight. The Saturday sun rendered baseless the ominous shadows of Friday night.

A silver 1978 MG zipped along the winding country road, flanked on both sides by rolling green hills and horse farms as far as the eye can see. Welcome to the Bluegrass region of Central Kentucky.

The sun had warmed the morning air enough that Cal lowered the top on his MG before hitting the backroads. They would eventually lead him to Halcott Farms where he intended to spend the morning exploring the grounds and chatting with chief of security John Hood.

A crisp April wind blew through Cal's hair as the silver convertible sped along the highway. Horses pawed at the ground behind black fences, tossing tails and nodding their majestic heads in greeting. They turned, watching as the car approached, passed, and then vanished in the distance.

A few miles outside of Lexington, the road opened up and the real estate of the city gave way to sparse countryside and huge estates. Mansions atop thousands of acres. Barns the size of movie theaters. These people own dozens—even hundreds—of horses that may not even race. For the millionaires of Woodford County, collecting horses is just something to do simply because they can.

Bourbon country. That's what the locals call this region of Kentucky. There are over a dozen operational distilleries within a 100-mile radius of Versailles, the seat of Woodford County. Not the least of which is Woodford Reserve which was churning out barrels of the aged brown liquid fewer than five miles from where Cal was headed. If this region's penchant for thoroughbreds was rivaled by anything, it was a stiff glass of 90-proof, single-barrel bourbon.

Cal was no stranger to Kentucky's drink of choice and as he approached Halcott Farms he couldn't help but fantasize a bit about the late Mr. Halcott's liquor cabinet, which he was sure stocked only the best of the best.

He figured he would know the Halcotts' entryway when he saw it and he was right. Though the mansion was not visible from the road, the massive iron gates blocking the driveway made it abundantly clear to any visitor the grounds they were about to enter. The gates were at least two stories tall and the hinges on which they hung looked powerful enough to sweep Cal's car from the road like a broom to a dust bunny.

Cal nudged the MG right up to the black gates and leaned over to press a button on the keypad to his left.

"Yes?" a gruff voice grumbled through the speaker.

"Cal Tyson to see Ms. Halcott."

No response, but a few seconds later he heard the mechanical lock trip and the gates slowly swung inward, revealing a winding driveway that was perfectly blacktopped and perfectly smooth. Cal shifted into first and slid through the gates, following the path through the meticulously manicured property.

The driveway split the middle of a small lake and entered a stretch of wooded pines. Huge fountains spewed on either side of Cal's convertible as he crossed the expanse of water and entered the wooded enclosure. Within seconds, the bright morning sun was blotted out behind thick pine trees that engulfed the drive. It was so dark under the trees Cal flipped on his headlights as he coasted through the woods.

The dense canopy gave an eerie impression of dusk even in the middle of day without a cloud in the sky. With the top down, Cal could hear hundreds of cicadas buzzing in the trees around him. The insect raucous enveloped the vehicle and drowned out even the purr of the car's engine. Pine needles filled his nostrils with the smell of wilderness.

"What am I getting myself into?" Cal mumbled as he crept through the forest. "A body could disappear out here and never be found again."

The trees reached over the top of the path. The trimmed branches met just overhead creating an arboreal tunnel through which the MG passed. Cal shifted into second and picked up the pace.

For nearly a mile the wooded pines pressed in upon the MG until suddenly Cal rounded a bend and the forest abruptly gave way to rolling hills. Sunlight flooded the forest opening and Cal squinted his eyes against the flash of brightness. The pine needle fragrance changed to the slightly sweet scent of freshly cut bluegrass.

There before Cal stood the most magnificent plantation mansion he had ever seen. Surely this was the set of a movie and not an actual home where people live just twenty miles outside of Lexington.

Cal knew the Halcotts' place was lavish, but he was not prepared for what lay ahead of him. The sterling white pillars alone were like giant redwood trees on either side of the veranda, stretching three stories into the sky and framing the fairytale entryway.

He pulled around the circular drive and parked in front of the massive staircase which spilled down to the driveway. Each stair was 80 feet long across and together they reminded Cal of bleachers at a college gymnasium except they were pure white marble and reached up to a solid wood double door that itself was the height of a normal house.

Cal killed the engine and stared up at the entryway wondering if he was even allowed to step on the pristine staircase. As he took the first step forward, one of the doors cracked open and an elderly gentleman appeared from behind the crest. He wore the suit of an old-fashioned butler complete with white gloves and tails.

"This has to be a joke," Cal muttered under his breath as he climbed the stairs toward the butler.

"Good morning, sir. Ms. Halcott is expecting you. Do come in," the man spoke as he sidestepped and held the giant wooden door ajar for Cal to enter.

If the exterior of the mansion was impressive, the interior was downright intoxicating. Polished marble as far as the eye could see. The walls were lined with paintings and tapestries. Sculptures and art of all kinds. Even the furniture was antique art. A braided Persian rug stretched wall to wall in the foyer and was at least 30 feet wide and 40 feet long.

Most impressive, though, was the split staircase which ascended both sides of the foyer and met 30 feet higher at the balcony overlooking the entryway. Just above Cal and the butler, flanked by the split staircase, was the most extravagant chandelier Cal had ever laid eyes on. The light fixture alone was worth more than he would make in a lifetime.

The butler directed Cal to a sitting room off the foyer and informed him Ms. Halcott would be down shortly. Then he quietly shuffled off to another wing of the mansion.

In the sitting room were Victorian era chairs and a fainting couch. Cal wasn't sure if sitting on the chair was against the rules, so he elected instead to stand in front of the twenty-foot windows which overlooked the expanse of the property.

Far in the distance, he saw a tractor pulling a mowing deck across the lush green grass. The rolling hills were mesmerizing, and Cal soon drifted into his thoughts.

It's hard to believe someone could sneak into this mansion and murder its inhabitant. A place like this probably requires a small army to keep up. Surely there are people awake and working around the clock here. Then again, with a monstrosity of this size, a gunshot in one wing might not even be audible in another.

He snapped back to reality when he heard footsteps padding down the marble staircase behind him and he wheeled around to greet the sound. What he saw rivaled the stunning magnificence of the diamond chandelier.

Harper Halcott paused about halfway down the staircase for what can only be described as a calculated performance. She wore a red silk kimono that stopped about four inches above her knee. It was loosely tied in front and left no secret about what was underneath. Her hair sat atop her head wrapped in a damp towel. A few loose strands escaped and hung across her pale cheek and down the back of her neck.

One bare foot was frozen a step higher than the rest of her body and the other was arched below her, raising her frame to balance, her hip resting against the banister.

She spotted Cal and smiled, clearly proud of the reaction she had elicited.

Cal blinked and pulled himself together.

"Late night?" he asked.

"Early morning."

She resumed her descent down the stairs.

"I love Saturday morning rides..." she trailed off.

Cal swallowed. "Well, you certainly have a beautiful place to do it."

"Thanks," she smiled cloyingly. "I hope you don't mind, but I've just stepped out of the bath and I didn't want to keep you waiting."

She waltzed across the foyer and perched on the fainting couch across from Cal and the window.

Cal didn't respond. The room was silent for a few moments until Harper spoke again.

"So what have you discovered so far? Any leads on my husband's murder?" She spoke the last word with a hint of sarcasm almost as though she intended to provoke.

"As a matter of fact I lined up an appointment with Jubal Early next week. I want to find out if he's involved, and I have a plan to get him to talk."

Harper seemed a bit surprised but listened intently.
"Do you think he's a suspect?"

"Too soon to tell really, but I'll know more on Monday. And by the way, I would prefer we don't throw the *M* word around just yet until we know who we can trust."

"Hmm. Well, I must say I'm impressed Mr. Tyson. You move fast..."

Was she flirting? Cal couldn't tell.

"Can I make you a drink, Cal? I'm having one."

As Harper spoke, she strolled across the floor and swung open the cabinet to reveal a hidden wet bar. Her pink toes left vanishing prints on the cold marble like breath steaming a window.

"I'd better not," he replied. But she was already standing in front of him, pressing the glass into his hand.

"Come on. It's the weekend. A little fun isn't going to *kill* you."

As she spoke, she leaned closer to Cal. He could smell the fresh lotion on her body. The scent was light and vaguely floral, lavender maybe. The kimono hung loosely over her curved breast.

Cal accepted the glass and their hands touched. Their eyes locked. Cal was losing the battle to remain objective.

"Ahem."

The voice from the foyer pierced the silence like a firecracker. Cal and Harper both jumped and stepped back.

A gruff man with a square jaw and a two-day stubble stood in the doorway. He wore a flannel shirt and blue jeans. His cowboy boots were caked with mud that had flaked on to the Persian rug beneath him.

Harper was the first to speak. "Oh, good morning, John. You startled me. How is the first mow of the season going?"

"Not bad, ma'am. It's good to be back on the grounds again."

Hood had a humble demeanor, but it was clear he was not to be messed with. He carried himself like a man who could hurt someone badly if he needed to and he wouldn't have a single regret about it.

"John, this is Mr. Cal Tyson. He's here to—"

"—I'm with the racing commission," Cal interrupted, extending his hand and walking toward Hood. "In light of the recent tragedy and publicity we would like to have a look around the grounds. You know, make sure everything is still on the level and ready for the big race next month."

"Oh, uh, sure," Hood grumbled.

"Yes, John, I'd like for you to show Mr. Tyson around this morning," Harper recovered. "Please grant him full access to all of the barns and answer any questions he might have."

"As you wish, ma'am."

She turned back to Cal. "Good to see you again, Mr. Tyson. Please don't be a stranger," she drawled. And with that, she whisked back up the stairs and disappeared around a corner.

The two men now stood alone in the foyer.

"I don't recall having a visit from the racing commission in years past, but I'm happy to show you around."

Cal noted the suspicion in Hood's tone.

"Great. Let's start with the barn that houses Valkyrie."

Hood led Cal through the winding hall to a side entrance off of the chef's kitchen. Outside, the noon sun had risen high overhead. The morning dew had evaporated into the atmosphere and with its infusion again came the pungent odor of freshly cut grass.

"You do security and landscaping both?" asked Cal.

"I manage everything that happens outside the walls of the house. If something enters or exits these grounds, rest assured I know about it. Of course, we have guys who do the grunt work and I oversee it."

"Aha, that makes sense. So you have an elaborate security system then, eh?"

"That would be an understatement. I'm sure you're aware of the value of this estate."

Cal decided to poke him a bit. "Not quite. What would you put it at ballpark?"

Hood grunted an inaudible response and slid into a farm utility vehicle parked next to the gardener's shed. Cal got the drift and took the passenger seat just as Hood floored the electric car in a spray of gravel. They sped down the track surrounding the private garden.

As they bumped along the gravel road, Cal gripped his seat to keep from being thrown out of the doorless vehicle. The noise from the rocks forced him to shout his questions.

"How long have you worked for the Halcotts, John?"

"Long time."

"You're not much of a talker, are you?" Cal asked, a bit perturbed.

Hood's face contorted with anger. He slammed on the brake and the vehicle skidded to a halt. They were deep within the acreage of the estate now and Cal could hear nothing but the sound of wind blowing over the hills and a distant lawn mower. Hood turned and faced him.

"Listen, pal, I don't know you and I don't know why you're here. All I know is the man I swore to protect died two weeks ago and it happened on my watch. Now, I realize there are rumors flying around about his death and the way I figure, it's not up to me to address them. That's the job of the police. I'm doing everything I can to salvage what dignity I have and lock this property down to any further monkey business. I will not lose another person nor animal within these fences, and every minute I have to spend playing Disney tour guide to you is a minute I'm not able to do what I'm trained for. So, I'll do exactly what Ms. Halcott wants. I'll answer your questions and I'll show you around and then I want you to get the hell out of here and leave me to my business. You got that?"

"Okay, I get it. Just making small talk," Cal groaned, trying to lighten the mood. It didn't work.

He made a mental note that Hood has an obvious anger problem.

Hood faced forward again and resumed the bumpy journey in silence. A few minutes later, they pulled up to a barn big enough to comfortably shelter a six-person family. The shrubs around it were immaculately manicured and there were a few stablehands milling about at the barn's opening.

No matter how well-maintained a stable, there is always manure. The unmistakable odor slapped Cal in the face as they parked the vehicle.

"This is where Valkyrie lives," Hood said. He swung his legs out of the Gator and made a beeline for the open barn door.

Cal followed behind within earshot and overheard the stablehands as they greeted Hood. Cal knew the horse farms around here often hire Irish immigrants to work with the horses, and judging by the accents, Halcott Farms also ascribed to that common practice.

"How is he today?" growled Hood to no one in particular.

"He had a good workout this marnin', sir," was the reply from a middle-aged man wearing mud-caked riding boots and holding a crop. "Did the ten furlongs in 2:01 flat."

"Goddamnit," spewed Hood. "I thought we weren't pushing him that hard this close to race day."

"We din't, sir. He opened up on his own, he did. Gave Kyna a real run fir her money. I swear't we might have a record on our hands. He runs like he wants it."

On cue, they heard a loud snort from inside the barn. Cal stepped inside and saw the subject of discussion raise its head repeatedly and stamp its hooves as though to acknowledge his understanding of the conversation.

Although it was only an animal, Cal sensed he was in the presence of greatness. The horse had charisma and he knew it. To Cal, it felt like meeting a movie star or a famous athlete. He actually felt the deference his body naturally offered to this impressive beast.

Valkyrie's color was pure black except for a single white fleck on his nose just below the eyes. As he moved, the animal's flesh rippled over solid muscles. Power was written over every inch of the horse's sovereign body.

"What a beautiful creature."

The Irishman chuckled and Cal realized he had spoken that last thought aloud.

"Not many a man sees 'im this close, mister. Consider yourself among the lucky." He nodded at Cal.

"How many people have direct access to this barn?" Cal asked.

Hood took over the conversation. "Other than the Halcotts and myself, maybe five other people. All devoted horse folk who love this horse and love the family they work for. I trust them all."

"Okay, but Harper mentioned something about Jubal Early snooping around recently?"

"For a racing commissioner, you sure ask a lot of questions."

"We have an open investigation on Early and his potential involvement in a doping scandal, so we're trying to collect as much information on him as we can," Cal lied.

That seemed to satisfy Hood.

"That no good sonofabitch got canned a few months back, but he couldn't take no for an answer. Kept showing up until I finally had to kick his ass out of here myself."

"So you didn't like Early? What was it about him?"

"He always seemed shady to me, but to be honest, it was Mr. Halcott who disliked him the most. The man of the house came to me one day and said Early was gone and that was that. Said I was never to allow Early on the property again. Apparently the two had some kind of disagreement or falling out and Mr. Halcott cut him off entirely."

"Any idea what the disagreement was about?"

"Not really. Mr. Halcott wasn't a man whose motives you questioned. I recall seeing them argue occasionally, but I couldn't tell you what about," Hood responded. "Do you guys think he was doping horses?"

"We're not at liberty to say just yet, but he's a person of interest. I appreciate your information."

Hood still seemed suspicious but less so now. Being in the presence of Valkyrie softened him up a little. He climbed back into the cart and swung around to pick up Cal.

The two Irishmen stood just inside the barn and watched the vehicle as it bounced back up the gravel road toward the house.

Hood took a roundabout way back to the front of the mansion and, as he did, he pointed out a few of the estate's main attractions. He was particularly proud of the hedgerow maze which, according to Hood, had been attempted by many a drunken reveler, but was never once solved.

"Designed and built it myself. Come back some time and see if you can solve it. I bet you'll never make it out," Hood challenged as he skidded to a halt next to the silver MG.

Cal wasn't so sure he ever wanted to be at the mercy of John Hood, garden maze or otherwise.

"Well, hope I was helpful," Hood announced. "Sorry if I come off rough. I take my job seriously."

"Life is far too important a thing ever to talk seriously about," Cal quipped as he cranked the MG's engine.

Hood stared blankly at him.

"Not an Oscar Wilde man I see," muttered Cal as he eased on to the blacktop driveway that would lead him back through the dense forest and out the iron gates.

Cal gassed the convertible and his mind drifted back to the red kimono. He didn't notice the BMW that slipped out from a side garage and fell into pace about 100 yards behind him.

11

Cal paused when he reached the giant gates. He waited for them to swing open and permit his exit. He was thinking about Hood and the conversation they had just had. Hood seemed like kind of an asshole, but he was one of those principled tough guys who would only kill you if you deserved it. Not the kind of guy who would turn on an employer or stab anyone in the back. No, Hood would look you right in the eye while he cracked your skull with a hammer.

He wasn't ready to clear Hood entirely though. Something about him bothered Cal. Was it the anger issue? The unflagging commitment to a sworn cause? The guy was clearly a little off no matter how you slice it.

Interesting news about Early, though. I'll have to see if I can provoke him to shed light on his falling out with Halcott, Cal thought as he drove.

The clock on his dash said 2:00 p.m. He cruised between the iron gates and turned right on the lonely road leading back to town.

The BMW from Halcott Estates also turned right a minute later, keeping pace with Cal's MG.

The warm spring afternoon had Cal in a good mood. He glanced over at a small creek that paralleled the road. He tried to remember the name. Elkhorn? No that's farther away from here, he recalled. Lots of good fishing holes in this part of the county. The Kentucky River is nearby. No doubt this stream flows into eventually. Cal's mind drifted.

Maybe I'll give Emma a call when I get back to town and see if she'd like to have dinner. Besides we need to figure out the game plan for Monday morning.

As Cal drove along the winding country road, he reached back to the first time he had seen Emma sitting behind the reference desk. He wondered if she was still reading Flannery O'Connor.

BAM!

The BMW gunned it and slammed into the back of Cal's car. He hadn't seen it coming at all and lurched forward veering off the road.

Cal regained control of the wheel and whipped off the shoulder back into his lane. He glanced in the rearview and saw the BMW was coming in for a second attempt. He hit the gas and shot forward just in time to avoid the second charge of his assailant.

"What the hell is going on?" Cal spoke aloud. "Did this guy come from the Halcotts? Has he been following me? What did I do to piss him off?"

Cal kept the pedal to the floor and managed to stay a few feet ahead of the speeding BMW. The country road was treacherous with winding curves and narrow bridges. Definitely not a good place for a high-speed car chase.

He looked again in the rearview, trying to get an ID on the driver. But the windows were tinted so dark it was impossible to see inside. He pulled his eyes back to the road and screeched around a 45-degree turn, spinning tires. The BMW was right behind him.

Just ahead Cal spotted a road sign announcing imminent danger. About 100 yards out and approaching rapidly.

GLENNS CREEK BRIDGE
NARROW CROSSING

On the other side of the bridge, he could see a box truck barreling toward him. The bridge would never be wide enough for two large vehicles to pass each other. But the MG was so tiny, he just might be able to sneak it past the big truck. It was his only hope. The BMW was bearing down on him. It was too late to stop now.

He swerved to the far right as he entered the bridge. The passenger mirror scraped the guardrail, sending sparks flying into the open convertible.

The oncoming truck's horn blared. Cal could see the terror in the driver's eyes. They would never make it.

The two cars met in the middle of the bridge and Cal leaned right. The MG swiped the bridge and his driver's side mirror clipped the speeding truck, but he barely squeaked past.

The BMW was not so lucky. It was too wide to execute the pass. Tires screeched and Cal's assailant slammed head on into the oncoming truck. The front end smashed in a terrible crash and the twisted metal careened over the side of the bridge into Glenns Creek below.

There's no way the driver of the BMW survived the crash, and Cal didn't wait around to find out. Both his side mirrors were smashed but he could see the smoking rubble as he adjusted his rearview with shaky hands.

Did Hood put a tail on him? That was more than a tail. They wanted him injured or worse. What did he do to provoke Hood's anger?

So many questions without answers. The MG was scraped up but still driving. Cal pulled himself together and continued toward town, regularly examining his rearview mirror for any evidence of another tail. Soon the expansive horse farms gave way to the familiar cityscape. The Lexington skyline loomed closer.

Cal scrapped the plan to meet Emma and instead decided to call his contact at the metro police department to run a background on Hood. This guy was more dangerous than Cal first thought.

He left the wrecked MG parked in an underground garage and rode the elevator to his seventh-floor office. If Hood had a hit out on him, he needed to act fast and protect himself.

He turned the key in his office door and stepped inside, closing and locking the door behind him. His .38 was in the desk drawer as always. He grabbed it and checked the clip.

Cal's friend Joe Brand was retired from the Metro Police Department after a 25-year career. He and Cal had met as training buddies at the YMCA and their similar personalities made them quick allies.

Despite Brand's long career in law enforcement, he was cynical of the institution. He occasionally lamented internal corruption and wasn't afraid to call out any of his colleagues who put their own interests above those of the community. Probably part of the reason he gave notice the day he hit 25 years.

"Brand here," spoke the voice on the other end of Cal's line after a half dozen rings.

"Hello, old friend. What took you so long—hanging out with your buddies in the sauna again?" Cal chided. They had a running joke about the old men who sat naked for hours in the YMCA locker room.

"Yeah, they asked about you, so I gave 'em your number."

"You sicko," Cal laughed. "Hey, on a serious note, do you recall ever having a run-in with a guy named John Hood?"

"Are you shitting me?"

"No. Why?"

"Yes, I know him. Tough guy? Ex-Ranger?"

"Sounds right. I wasn't aware he was former military. How do you know him?"

"He applied to the force at least three times. No trouble with the physical requirements, but he failed the psych eval every time."

"You don't say? What for?"

"OK, this is off the record, you know, but the dude was psycho. Bad anger problems and super paranoid. He thought everyone was out to get him. Cadets have to run a mile during the physical and a couple of them laughed about something god knows what. Well, Hood, snapped on one of the guys. Thought for sure they were making fun of him and he beat the poor guy within an inch of his life. I mean, he went crazy. That was the last we ever heard of Hood."

"Very interesting," Cal drawled. "He's running security out at Halcott Farms now and I'm pretty sure he just tried to have me killed."

"Damn, buddy. Don't tell me the details because I don't want to be involved but watch yourself with that guy. He ain't right in the head and you don't want to get on his bad side. Who knows what kind of shit those Rangers did over in Iraq. I know he was there. Keep away from him is my advice."

"I'll do my best. I appreciate the inside info, man. Don't linger too long in that sauna."

"Damn you," Brand deadpanned. "Meet me there sometime and I'll whip your ass at racquetball again."

Cal chuckled and hung up the phone.

Hood is a loose cannon, eh? That explains a lot. Looks like he's back on the list of prime suspects.

12

Bright and early Monday morning, Cal pulled into the Kenwick neighborhood of East Lexington in search of 288 Bassett Avenue. This part of downtown is known for its literary culture and artistic types, so he wasn't surprised when Emma told him he would find her here.

The MG came to rest in front of a quaint mid-century style, single-story house with a Craftsman front porch. Flower-filled planters on either side of the steps splashed pinks, purples, and yellows across the entryway. Nothing too fancy, but cozy, clean, and a little quirky.

A gray cat lounged lazily on the front walk. It rolled on its back and turned its eyes up to Cal as he approached.

"Meow."

Cal reached down and scratched the cat's head.

"Do you live here, fella?"

The tip of the cat's tail flicked like a metronome. Faint hint of kibble and cat litter.

Cal straightened his back, stretched, and stepped up on to the front porch.

Emma answered the door in jeans and a sweater with a knitted wool scarf wrapped around her neck and slung over her shoulder. She leaned forward and gave Cal a hug on the porch and, as she did, her long blond hair fell back to reveal a playful set of large earrings. They had a vaguely African vibe that elicited a sophisticated tone from the otherwise nondescript outfit. She looked comfortable and intelligent. And sexy too.

Cal was the first to speak.

"Nice place you've got here."

"Why, thank you. It's nothing fancy, but I love it. I've wanted to live in this neighborhood since I moved to Lexington."

"Well, maybe next time I can get the full tour, but now we'd better hit the road if we are going to be on schedule to meet Jubal."

He turned and headed for the stairs leading down to the sidewalk. She didn't follow. He glanced back.

"Are we taking that?" she asked, nodding toward the road.

"Uh, what else do you have in mind?"

"Listen, I like the MG and all, but in case you haven't noticed, it looks like it went through a garbage disposal."

"Right. That. I can explain on the way. Unless you have another option?"

Emma was already rounding the corner into her driveway and heading for the garage. Cal stayed put, waiting.

He heard the garage door open and then the sound of a revving engine. From around the side of the house appeared Emma behind the wheel of a bright yellow Porsche Boxster. It was a beauty.

"Are you going to get in or just stand there and gawk?"

"How on earth can you afford a Porsche like this on a librarian's salary?" Cal asked incredulously.

"Hey, I told you I went to private school. My parents take care of their daughter, what can I say," she smirked. "But don't worry—I'm not spoiled. I paid for grad school the old-fashioned way. Bartending and student loans."

Cal chuckled. He believed her. She came off as a down to earth gal, and he never got the impression she felt entitled to anything.

He guessed it would be good to have a partner who is comfortable around big money. God knows he wasn't.

He shrugged and hopped in the Porsche. Emma zipped out on Richmond Road and headed for the interstate.

"So, about my car," Cal said as the Porsche hit the onramp for I-64W.

Emma shifted into fifth and opened up the throttle.

"I paid a visit to the Halcott Estate on Saturday and somebody wasn't happy about it."

Emma reached for the volume knob and turned down the radio before responding.

"First of all, *you went to the Halcott mansion*? O-M-G," Emma stated dramatically. "And, second, are you saying someone tried to hurt you?"

"Yes to both. I even saw Valkyrie in the flesh. And then a mysterious henchman chased me out of the county and smashed my car up." Cal decided to leave out the gruesome details of the fiery accident.

"This is too crazy. I can't believe what I'm hearing." Then she realized the gravity of the situation and became visibly uncomfortable. She hesitated. "Are we in danger right now?"

"I don't believe so. No one knows I'm with you and, besides, we're in your car. I'm sure we are fine."

The look on Emma's face betrayed both her excitement and fear. Cal changed the subject.

"You should have seen that horse. Truly amazing animal. One of the stablehands said he might even be capable of breaking Secretariat's record from 1973."

"I'm so jealous. What was the house like? Did you see Harper Halcott?" Emma turned in her seat to quiz Cal.

He thought she said Harper's name with slight disdain. Was that judgment in her tone?

"I could never begin to describe the house. Just take your wildest dreams and multiply them by ten. I can't believe there are places like that in Kentucky."

Harper pulled something from her pocket and extended her fist to Cal.

"Here."

She opened her palm to reveal a silver wedding band.

Cal laughed nervously and took the ring. It was a little loose on his finger, but it did the job.

"I do?" he questioned facetiously.

She slid a diamond ring on her own left hand. Cal decided it was best not to ask.

"Better watch that tone or we'll stop by my parents' house for dinner and show you off." She smiled slightly and slammed the car into sixth gear.

They drove in silence for a while. Both assumed the other was thinking about that last statement.

Finally, Cal broke the quiet.

"Jubal thinks we're from Bowling Green and we are looking to train a prize horse for next year. Our angle is we're unknown but have the capital to invest with the right people."

"I can handle that."

"I'm going to try and push him to find out why he left the Halcotts. See if he admits to harboring any ill will toward them."

"OK, you think he might have killed Sterling?"

"It's possible. There certainly seems to be motive if Halcott fired him recently. I also want to know if he saw any funny business going on in the stables, but that might be harder to pull off given our aliases."

"I'm game. We'll see what we can do."

They cruised along I-64 until the skyscrapers of downtown Louisville rose to their left. Emma hung a right and hit the bridge that crossed the Ohio River and led to the Jeffersonville exit.

13

The majestic skyline of Louisville faded quickly once Cal and Emma crossed the bridge to Jeffersonville. This peripheral town was where the blue-collar workers of the larger city lived. The maids and garbage men. The waiters and mechanics. The strippers and construction workers. Across the bridge where the real estate was cheaper. You want to be in Louisville but can't afford it, you buy a place in Jeffersonville and commute.

Because of its reputation as an affordable alternative to Derby city, the town drew flocks of people with big dreams and small budgets. And the landscape reflected it. Pawn shops and payday lenders lined the streets. A rundown bar on every corner. The predominant color of the town was neon.

Emma and Cal stuck out in the yellow Porsche as they cruised down Riverside Drive looking for the diner where they planned to meet Jubal Early.

"Remind me to come here next time I need to dispose of a body," Cal joked, nodding toward the docks just to their left on the Ohio River.

The docks were alive with movement on Monday morning as men unloaded a ship laden with huge metal containers. Screeching sounds of scraping metal and grinding gears as a couple of rusted cranes lowered the shipping containers on the platform below. The air was musty and damp. It smelled like the city itself was sweating into a pit-stained undershirt.

They spotted the Triple Crown Diner tucked away near the I-65 overpass. It was a typical greasy spoon nestled near a bend in the river. The back of the diner was lined with windows that overlooked the water and framed the horizon of the big city across it.

The joint looked like a good place to eat breakfast, but there was no denying the gloomy air that permeated the landscape. It was a desperate strip and the people who frequented it were not accustomed to financial security or good homes. This part of town emitted a no bullshit vibe and that sentiment was reflected in the eyes of the people Cal and Emma passed on the street.

It was 10:00 a.m. on the dot when they slid into a parking spot in back of the Triple Crown.

In a corner booth sat a middle-aged man with gray hair slicked back over his forehead. His skin was weathered and brown. Deep creases around his eyes and mouth. His large forearms extended from the rolled-up sleeves of a wrinkled button-down. His arms rested on the table in front of him, which was littered with an assortment of open newspapers.

Cal recognized Early from the Courier-Journal photo he had seen at the library. As they made their way toward the table, Early looked up. He slowly folded the newspapers and set them to the side. Cal spotted various incarnations of the daily racing forms which offered expert picks and insider information on the day's meets.

"Hello, Mr. Early. I'm Cap Barclay and this is my wife—" Cal panicked when he suddenly realized Emma didn't yet have an alias name.

"—I'm Victoria. Victoria Barclay," Emma quickly interjected. "My husband likes to pretend he makes the decisions around our farm, but we all know the truth." She smiled and winked at Jubal.

Early nodded and extended his hand to them both. "Nice to meet you. I've always found the lady of the house to have a sixth sense when it comes to equine affairs. No offense, Mr. Barclay."

"None taken, old boy!" Cal surprised even himself with the absurd accent he suddenly affected. He thought this particular alias called for a Jay Gatsby meets William Faulkner style persona.

"How's Keeneland looking this week?" he asked, indicating toward the racing form in Early's left hand.

"No races on Monday, of course, but the Bluegrass Stakes is Saturday. Big money riding on that heat," Early answered Cal's question, but continued holding his gaze on Emma. She feigned a blush and slid into the booth across from him.

Cal couldn't help admiring the way Emma had already set the tone of the conversation and coaxed Early to lower his guard.

"So you're the man with the plan when it comes to racehorses, is that right?" Cal got down to business.

"Some say," Early responded curtly. "But I don't work for just anyone anymore. I've had bad luck training horses for assholes. Pardon my language, ma'am."

"Understood. I'd be lying if I said we didn't do our research. You had been working for the Halcott family until just recently, correct?" Cal prodded.

Early nodded.

Emma pushed him for more. "What's Harper like? I've seen her on TV. Excuse me for saying, but I have a theory she's a bit of a bitch…" As she spoke, she leaned in and lowered her voice, laughing good-naturedly as she uttered the final word.

Early's eyes flashed. She'd hit on something.

"Listen, it's a real shame what happened to Halcott, but to be honest, I never liked either one of 'em. They didn't know a goddamn thing about training horses, and they didn't care to learn. Just wanted to push the animals as hard as possible, regardless of the horse's health. Make as much money as they could and then move on to the next one."

"So they mistreat their horses?" Cal asked.

"Depends on who you ask I guess. The whole industry is motivated by money, so there's a natural inclination to push everything to the limit."

Early seemed genuinely disappointed with the trend he described. "Not me, though. I care about the horses I train, and I never push them harder than they can handle."

"And that was the source of your disagreement with the Halcotts?"

"For the most part. Valkyrie is a real athlete. He will go down in the history books and be remembered forever, if they don't blow out his legs first. It makes me sad to lose my connection to him, but I refuse to hurt an animal for my own personal gain."

Cal and Emma exchanged a quick glance.

"You quit on your own accord then?" Cal probed.

Early grunted his assent.

Cal paused. But Harper and John Hood both said they *fired* Early. He wanted to know more but couldn't ascertain a way to press it without exposing himself.

"Very well. We would like to invite you to our property in Bowling Green sometime in the next few months to see if you would be interested in joining the staff and helping us train a future Derby winner. What do you think about that?"

"No harm in talking, but I ain't cheap."

"I wouldn't expect otherwise," Cal replied. "You will be handsomely rewarded for your services should we elect to hire you."

"Judging by the Porsche you rolled up in, I'd say you can afford me." Early nodded out the window and ventured a grin.

Emma nudged Cal's knee under the table.

"While we're here," Cal said, "I wonder if you know anything about our competition. I understand Augusto Gallo has a few Derby hopefuls in his stables down south."

"I know the South American prick, but he can't beat me. I saw him visit the Halcotts a few times while I was training Valkyrie. Seems like an uptight asshole. I heard his stables in Argentina are a sight to see. He's a real big wig down there. But I'll take talent over money any day."

"You aren't short on confidence I see, old sport," Cal replied. "I like that in a man. I look forward to working with you. We will be in touch soon to make further arrangements for your visit."

"Fine. Nice to meet you."

As Early spoke, he patted Emma's hand and smiled wide enough to reveal a gold cap in his back right molar. She nodded, returned the affectation, and rose to leave.

Cal hovered at the table for a second as Emma stood up. "Hey, I have to ask—Jubal Early? Any relation to the Civil War General? I fancy myself a bit of a history buff and I couldn't help noticing the connection."

"Great Uncle four generations removed. He was a good man with great ideas and I'm proud to carry his lineage." Early sat up and straightened his shoulders as he reflected on his distant relative.

"I see. Wasn't he a proponent of the Lost Cause of the Confederacy?"

"Is this a business meeting or a history lesson?" Jubal barked. "What most people don't realize is the Civil War was a battle over state's rights." He paused momentarily to let the statement sink in.

"How much did you pay the federal government in taxes last year?" Early continued. "If the South had won the Civil War, it would have been a lot less. And we wouldn't be writing checks to keep people on welfare. Bunch of entitled deadbeats taking our hard-earned living away."

Cal remained silent.

Early continued, "You're obviously a wealthy southern man. You can't tell me you prefer to have those idiots in Washington controlling the way we do business here in Kentucky. We do things differently in the South and we should be able to legislate and govern our states autonomously."

Early was working himself into a frenzy. Cal had clearly opened a door he didn't want to walk into. He knew the "state's rights" argument was almost always a slippery slope that led to some kind of bigoted punchline. Living in the south had taught him to be leery of anyone who starts down that path.

"Yes, I see where you're coming from," was all Cal could muster. "Well, I recognized the name and couldn't help wondering."

But Early wasn't letting go. "Listen, if you're a believer, you should come to one of our meetings. Good group of guys gets together a few blocks from here the first Tuesday of every month. We'd be glad to have another member. I can get you on the email list?"

"Hmm...let me send you my contact info. Sounds interesting," Cal pacified.

Early nodded and stared up from the table dumbly.

Cal extended his hand for a shake and the two left Early right where they had found him, alone at the table with his racing forms.

Once outside, Cal leaned over to Emma and said, "Not bad there, Victoria. Not bad at all."

She smiled and quietly snickered as she unlocked the Porsche and climbed inside. "You weren't so bad yourself, Colonel Sanders. Where the heck did that accent come from?"

He laughed. "I was quietly hating myself the whole time, but it seemed to work. Once I started, there was no going back."

Emma fired up the engine. "How bout that lecture you just got? Dude was off his rocker, right?"

"Yeah, and I'm sure he will be the guy representing the South on CNN next week. Why do the crackpots always become spokespeople for our region? Guys like him make us all look bad. What a nutjob."

"Seriously."

Emma cut the wheel and backed out of the parking spot.

As the car pulled parallel to the restaurant, they could see into the window to the table they had just left. Early's eyes stared vacantly at them. He was watching. Emma quickly looked away. She shuddered. "Ew, freak."

Early continued watching the car as they drove away until it vanished behind the I-65 overpass.

"Hey, it's a nice day. Might as well enjoy it since we're up here, right?" challenged Emma as she skipped the exit for 64 east and instead got off in downtown Louisville.

Cal shrugged silently and acquiesced. Not like he had anything else to do today. He was along for the ride.

They headed south on 3rd Street through Old Louisville and then past the University of Louisville campus, where students were bustling about in preparation for the last two weeks of classes.

As they drove, downtown slowly faded into the background and the landscape turned more and more residential.

Louisville is a city in geographical crisis. While it is located in the southern state of Kentucky, it is just across the river from Illinois and Indiana, both northern states. It is a city of industry fueled by the Ohio River that slices through it. Perhaps more than any other city in America, influences of both the northern and southern cultures are prominently on display. One neighborhood is quaint and friendly, the next is tough and hardboiled, scarred by graffiti and crime. It is constantly hanging in the balance of Northern pragmatism and Southern gentility.

Emma slapped Cal's knee and pointed out the windshield. Smack in the middle of Central Avenue stood Churchill Downs in all its glory.

Though he had been a Kentuckian for several years now, Cal had never actually seen the famous track. He was surprised at how residential the area surrounding the racetrack was. There were houses and tree-lined streets and then, bam, right in the middle of town was the most storied racetrack in history.

In less than a month, this strip would be completely unnavigable. On that special Saturday in May, there would be cars parked everywhere and drunken tailgaters as far as the eye can see.

"I had no idea this place was right in the middle of a neighborhood," Cal said as they passed the parking lot entrance.

"Wait—you mean you have never been to the Derby?" Emma was shocked by Cal's admission.

"Nope."

"Oh my gosh. It's totally insane, but everyone should experience it at least once."

"Decadent and depraved, right?" Cal referenced the famous Hunter S. Thompson gonzo journalist account of the 1970 running.

"Yes, and I love every minute of it. My parents actually have a box, but they rarely go in anymore. If you play your cards right, this might just be your year," she smirked.

They hung a left away from the racetrack and veered toward Baxter Avenue.

"I know a good place to have lunch near Cherokee Park, if you're game?"

"Why not," Cal replied.

There was no denying he had developed a bit of a crush on her. He knew it was probably trouble, but he just couldn't help it.

14

Emma squeezed into a parking spot against the curb of bustling Bardstown Road.

"This is one of my favorite places on earth," she said, gesturing around them at the populated street lined with dive bars, hip restaurants, and quaint coffee shops. "You can find anything you want here."

Cal was a little ashamed he hadn't explored this part of Louisville before. He knew the Bardstown Road strip was a popular hot spot and he had planned to visit several times before but had never gone through with it. Anyway, he was glad to have a tour guide for his first visit. He was used to traveling alone, so being in the presence of good company was a nice change of pace.

It was noon when the pair entered Rainey's Cafe which, according to Emma, had one of the best lunches in Louisville. When the door opened the intoxicating smell of exotic spices and incense wafted out on to the sidewalk. It filled their nostrils and foreshadowed the atmosphere of the restaurant they were about to enter. They opted for a table in the front window where they could watch people walk past on the busy sidewalk.

"So?" Emma raised her eyebrows and leaned into the table.

"So what?"

"Jubal! Get your head in the game, man. Let's talk. Is he suspicious?"

"I like how you have staked your claim on this case already. You're a regular dick now, aren't you?" He smiled at his own joke.

"Is that what they call *female* P.I.s, too? I do not approve."

"Lady dick?"

"No. Just no. I'm shutting this down right now." She shook her head in disapproval. "Wasn't it creepy how he watched us drive away?"

"I'll give you that. He's not a person I want to be friends with. He's a creep for sure. But I don't know if he is our guy."

"Why not?"

"Well, for starters he has too much compassion for animals to be a killer," Cal responded. "Cold-blooded murderers don't typically carry on about animal rights. That's our first tip."

"I hear you. What else?"

"He made no effort to hide his disdain for the Halcotts. If you kill somebody, you at least pretend to tolerate them so as to throw people off your scent. Early might be a strange bird, but he is smart enough to know better than to trash talk a man he just murdered."

"You think he's clear then? What about all the weird Civil War ranting?"

"I'm not quite ready to completely exonerate him, but I will say I would be surprised if he is the murderer. That being said, God knows what else he's guilty of. I don't really want to find out. Personally, I hope I never see the guy again."

"Me too," Emma concurred.

The waiter greeted them, and they ordered lunch from the menu. The restaurant had about every country in the world represented in its cuisine.

The waiter took their order to the kitchen, leaving Cal and Emma alone again. They sat quietly, both staring out the window and watching the people of Louisville wander the strip. It was a pretty day and the sidewalks were packed with people.

After a while Emma spoke again.

"But this isn't a total dead end, though, right? Who is Augusto Gallo? He sounds familiar. That seemed worth looking into."

Cal smiled. Yes, she was good.

"Completely agreed. In fact, when I first met with Harper, she listed Gallo as a possible suspect in her husband's murder," he responded. "I figured Jubal knew of him, but I didn't expect to hear about Gallo's visits to Halcott Farms. That caught me off guard."

Emma was listening.

"He's a big-time breeder down in Argentina. Apparently, he races horses up here in the states, and he obviously knew Sterling Halcott well enough to visit him at home."

"Right, I knew I recognized the name. I remember seeing him on TV now," said Emma. "He looks like a cocaine kingpin. Like a classy one who makes his henchmen do all the dirty work while he sips espresso on his vineyard the size of Connecticut."

"You're probably closer to the truth than you realize. I've heard rumors."

"Um hm. So when is our flight to Buenos Aires?"

Cal nearly choked on the last bite of his sandwich.

Emma smiled. "I'll let you buy my plane ticket later, but for now you can start with lunch."

She hopped up from the table and excused herself to the ladies' room.

It was such a pretty afternoon when they stepped outside of Rainey's they decided to go for a walk and enjoy the weather. Cherokee Park, the biggest green space in the city, was right around the corner. They popped into a coffee shop for a cup to go and hung a left on Cherokee Parkway, where they strolled leisurely toward the park.

They both realized this was becoming more like a date and less like a business meeting. The pace of their conversation was changing. Their tones were shifting. Softer, but with a little more sarcasm. Some might call it flirting.

As they entered the grounds of the park, they stopped to observe a huge stone statue of John Breckinridge Castleman perched atop a triumphant steed.

Erected 1913
In Honor of
John Breckinridge Castleman
Born June 30 1841 — Died May 23 1918
By friends who loved and respected him as a noble patriot, a
gallant soldier, a useful citizen, and an accomplished gentleman.
Major C.S.A.
Brigadier General U.S.A.

"Wow check that out. Pretty cool," Cal said and pointed at the nameplate.

He and Emma studied the statue.

"Wait a sec. C.S.A.? Does that stand for…"

"Confederate States of America," Emma finished his thought.

"How about that?" Cal whistled.

"Yeah, and get this," Emma broke in, "he was *exiled* from the country after the Civil War. It wasn't until a year later that Andrew Johnson pardoned him so he could return."

"Seriously? Exiled?" Cal couldn't believe it. He remembered Emma had written her master's thesis on the antebellum south.

"Yep, and now he is commemorated with one of the most famous statues in Louisville," she trailed off. "The South, man. The South. Got to love it."

The thing is she wasn't being sarcastic. Cal felt it, too. He knew the South had a strange history, but southerners couldn't help feeling pride for it—even while rejecting the ideals on which that history was largely based. The conflicted Southern identity.

"Oh, look! What's going on up there?!" Emma was excited as she pointed toward the park.

Sure enough, they had apparently picked a good day for a stroll. Some kind of carnival was set up on the grounds of the usually serene green space. The festivities were complete with vendors and games of chance and even an eclectic assortment of carnies wearing clown makeup, walking on stilts, and juggling as they milled about the grassy area.

"Oh boy," Cal said. His tone betrayed his reservations.

"Come on, old man. Let's at least get some ice cream and wander around for a bit. It'll be fun."

She grabbed Cal's hand and dragged him into the swirling crowd.

15

"Come win your lady a prize!" the huckster shouted at Cal as they wandered through the maze of tents and food trucks.

Cotton candy, kettle corn, funnel cakes. Fried food and sugar on all sides. The air smelled like a deep-fried twinkie.

"Step right up!"

The carney was standing in front of a booth that challenged players to shoot out the center of a target with pellets fired from a child-sized bb gun.

"All you have to do is shoot out the target, sir! Any halfway decent man could do it! What's the matter—scared you might embarrass yourself?" he called out as they walked past.

"Scared, eh?" Emma chided.

"Please. I could shoot circles around that dude," Cal answered coolly.

"Oh, what a badass," Emma teased. Then she thought for a second and switched gears. "Just out of curiosity, do you carry a gun?"

"Wouldn't you like to know."

"Hey, I just like to be warned when a man is about to point his weapon at me."

Cal slowly shook his head good-naturedly. He polished off the last bite of the ice cream they were sharing and tossed the empty cup into a trash can.

"Come here."

He put his arm around her shoulder and pulled her in close to him.

Emma made no effort to resist the bold move. She leaned into the crook of his arm. He felt a rush of excitement. Here goes nothing. We have crossed the threshold now.

Throngs of people filtered past the pair as they stood frozen in the middle of the path. No one seemed to notice them. Cal took her face in his hands and bent down. As he did, Emma raised her chin and pursed her lips to meet his. They kissed.

"Ding!" rang a bell behind them as someone slammed a rubber mallet down on the High Striker.

Emma and Cal pulled away and laughed at the coincidence.

"How about that for a first kiss?" Cal asked, continuing to stare into Emma's eyes.

"Right. You can go pay that bell ringer the five bucks you promised him now," she teased as she released her grip and took a step forward.

Ahead of them a crowd had gathered around a particularly boisterous showman who was running a version of the shell game with coconuts and a rubber ball.

"Easiest game in the world!" he called to the masses. "Watch the hands, follow the ball! Double your money in 30 seconds! One good eye and you're a winner! No tricks, no gimmicks! Step right up and put your money on the table!"

Cal and Emma stood at the back of the crowd, watching the trick unfold with mild interest.

On the table, dollar bills were flying around as fast the man could swap his coconuts. Within a few seconds, Cal had become mesmerized by the repetitive motion of the man's hands as they slid across the table. The little rubber ball appeared and then vanished under another coconut, appeared again and then vanished.

Cal's eyes became entranced and his focus slipped away.

He needed to arrange a meeting with Augusto Gallo. But how? That is not exactly the kind of guy you just call up on the phone. He had no doubt Harper would cover his expenses, but could he just show up in Buenos Aires expecting to chat with Gallo? No way that is happening. So far, all signs are pointing to Gallo as a person of interest. He had to figure out a way to talk with him.

Emma broke his trance. "Do you see that guy standing behind the table? He keeps looking at us. It's kind of creeping me out," she said. "Anyway, why is he even back there? He can't see the game from that angle. He's standing behind the action."

Cal looked in the direction she was indicating. He froze when he realized who she was pointing at.

It was the man in the grey suit he had seen that night at McIntyre's! The guy was wearing sunglasses that hid his sightless eye, but Cal could see the scar extending above the dark lens to his forehead and below to his upper lip.

"Keep it cool. No need to panic, but I think we have a secret admirer," he whispered into Emma's ear.

"Wait, you know that guy?" she asked. A tinge of fear crept into her tone and her demeanor became more frantic.

"Yeah. I'm not sure it's anything to worry about, but let's get out of here."

He tapped her elbow and cut a swath through the crowd of people behind them.

Emma didn't ask any questions. She followed Cal's lead and fought to keep up against the current of people pressing in the opposite direction. She glanced back over her shoulder.

"He's coming!" Her voice was verging on panic now.

Cal turned to see the man in the grey suit pushing through the crowd toward them. Cal picked up the pace and reached his hand under his jacket to unclip the holster that held his .38.

They escaped the crowd and ducked behind a taco truck on the outskirts of the fairgrounds.

"What do we do? Who is that guy?" Emma asked once she caught her breath.

"To be totally honest, I'm not sure. But I intend to find out," Cal answered. "Now let's get back to the car and go home before we see him again." Cal was already heading for the car as he spoke.

They kept a quick pace the whole way back to the Porsche, both of them throwing looks backward to be sure they had lost their tail. Neither relaxed until they were pulling out into the traffic of Bardstown Road.

"I thought you said we were safe!" Emma exclaimed once they were in the clear.

"I don't know how that guy found us or why. This case is getting more dangerous every day. Obviously, there are people who don't want me poking around in their business."

"As much as I hate to say it, that is probably all the more reason you should be," Emma responded cautiously.

Cal looked over at her but didn't answer. He watched quietly as she shifted gears and merged on the interstate that would lead them back to Lexington.

16

Nine days had passed since his visit to Louisville, and Cal was no closer to cracking the case. He had not even gotten a break on the identity of the man in the grey suit. The Kentucky Derby was only two weeks away.

He had been asking around regarding the sudden appearance in town of a man with a scar across one eye, but no one else had seen him, let alone had any insight on his whereabouts. Even the usually reliable former detective Joe Brand was coming up empty this time.

As far as Cal knew, the only people who had even laid eyes on this mysterious visitor other than himself were Emma and the bartender from McIntyre's. But Cal had seen him in both Lexington *and* Louisville. And both times the guy seemed to be following him. It was definitely enough to make a man suspicious.

He couldn't dwell on the past for long. The week ahead would take all of his focus. Saturday would mark the opening day of the debaucherous streak leading up to the Derby. Dozens of parties kicked off in Louisville this weekend, many of which would continue throughout the entire week until the night of the main event.

Cal had caught one lucky break. The most famous pre-party of the season fell on opening Saturday each year, and he had it on good authority Augusto Gallo was set to attend. Now he just needed to get on that guest list and create an alias that would allow him to get close enough to Gallo to have a chat.

Harper was his only hope of getting on the list for this exclusive party. Most of these shindigs had a vaguely charitable motive and attendees made the cut mostly because they had donated somewhere in the neighborhood of six figures to the nonprofit du jour the event was allegedly sponsoring. He needed Harper to work her magic and sneak him in.

What would be the best disguise for an event like this? Cal pondered the question as he dialed the Halcott's private line. Better keep it low-key. Something relatively anonymous that no one would bother to question.

"Hello?" The usually calm and collected Harper sounded uncharacteristically frazzled.

"Harper?"

"Hello? Who's there?" She was practically shouting through the receiver to be heard over some kind of loud commotion in the background.

Cal couldn't make out the source of the noise. He raised his voice to match the volume of his conversant.

"Harper, it's Cal Tyson," he spoke loudly. "What in the hell is going on out there?"

"Oh! Hiya, Cal!" she responded in a more friendly tone. "Don't mind the noise. It's the annual visit from our

100

friends at PETA. We have a few hundred protestors in the front lawn, complete with all of the local news media. You should see it out here. We've got naked people. We've got handcuffs. We've got saddles. Baby, we've got it all."

"I can only imagine," Cal replied. "How do they get on your private property? That doesn't seem fair."

"Sterling always figured it was better to allow them one good day of protesting in the open than to have to put up with secret attacks all year long. He had a name for it—something about a Russian philosopher…Bactine? Does that sound right? It all made sense at the time. But now…" She trailed off as she reflected on the memory of her late husband.

Cal tried to change the subject. "Listen, the Bonnycastle Gala is coming up this Saturday and I was wondering if you plan to attend?"

"Hold on, hon. I can barely hear you," Harper shouted. "I'm going to another room."

Cal hung on the line and gradually heard the din of the crowd subside as Harper moved further into the house.

"OK, that's better. Is that better?" she finally asked.

"Much better," Cal replied. His right ear was still ringing from the noise. He realized he had been pressing the receiver hard against it in order to make out Harper's words.

"Oh, good. Here I am relegated to my bathroom in order to have a conversation in my own home. Isn't that funny?" she asked. "I'm sitting in my bathroom to talk on the phone. Sterling would never have allowed this to happen. He would have marched out there and told them to give us some peace."

Cal remained quiet and waited for her to continue.

"I'm sorry, I'm sorry. I do miss him, though. We worked so hard to maintain a professional persona in the public eye. But we cared for each other—we really did. Now he's gone forever. Sometimes I get so sad."

"That's perfectly reasonable, ma'am. I don't blame you at all." Cal had never been great with crying women.

"Ma'am?! Oh, don't you dare ma'am me," Harper retorted. She quickly regained her composure. "Ma'am? You jerk!" she chided and managed a small laugh. "If you ever say that to me again, I'll throw you to the angry PETA horde."

Cal chuckled. "My apologies. Never again."

"Good. Now what is it you are wanting? The Bonnycastle party. Yes, I will be there. Have to keep up appearances, of course."

"I'm hoping to get some face time with Augusto Gallo and rumor has it he will be in attendance."

"I can get you in the party, but I can't promise you will be able to meet Augusto. He's a secretive sucker and he usually has an entourage surrounding him at big events like this."

"Hmm…but it's worth a shot at least," Cal replied. He decided to test Harper a little with the information he learned from Jubal Early. "Have you personally met Gallo?"

She seemed a bit flustered. "Um, yes, I believe so. He, uh, I think he's been to our house to visit Sterling before."

Cal saw through the guarded response. She was hiding something, but he decided not to press it until he had more to go on.

"Just wondering if you would be able to introduce us, should the opportunity arise on Saturday."

She exhaled slightly.

"Oh, yes, darling. I'll do my best. Now surely you don't want me to use your real name on this guest list, do you?"

"No, I don't think that would be wise. Let's go with something ambiguous and boring. I don't want any questions about whether I belong."

"Everyone will be so drunk on their own egos, no one will notice you. Oh, and don't forget about the booze," she laughed.

"Good to know, but still, an incognito and ubiquitous professional persona is better. Let's go with...hmm...Frank Diamond, entrepreneurial investor."

"Whatever you say, baby. Diamond: party of one."

"Ahem. Better make that party of two. Mr. and Mrs. Diamond."

"Oh, you don't say? And who might be the lucky Mrs. Diamond?" Harper teased.

"Just a friend. I've found people are more relaxed around married men. It tends to make them more open." He felt his face growing hot with embarrassment.

"Riiiiight. Very well, then. Mr. and Mrs. Diamond will both be welcome at the Bonnycastle mansion on Saturday."

"Thank you, Harper. I appreciate your help and I will see you then."

"Um hm," was her only reply before abruptly hanging up.

He sat in his desk chair and stared vacantly at the phone he had just been holding. On his notepad, he wrote:

— *Frank Diamond*
— *Startup investor*

— Latest acquisitions:

He tapped his pen on the desk. Glanced out the window. Stood and walked over to the percolating coffee pot on his credenza. He withdrew the carafe from the drip and poured a steaming cup of black coffee.

Cup in hand, he paced the room, stopping to stare out the window on Vine Street below. He returned to his desk and sat back down.

—Latest acquisitions:

His mind was blank. I need some inspiration. Maybe Lady Diamond will have some ideas.

He took a sip of coffee and dialed Emma's number.

17

"Imagine you are a venture capitalist and you are looking for a startup business to invest in."

Cal skipped the pleasantries and immediately started talking when he heard Emma's voice.

"OK, I'm listening," she replied somewhat skeptically. Her tone indicated she was caught off guard, but curious.

"You have a million dollars to spend on any business you like. What sticks out to you right now?"

"Man, you are a weird one, aren't you?"

"I'm sure it's part of my charm. Well?"

"First of all, I would like to state for the record I hope to never be referred to as a venture capitalist again. It sounds gross."

"Duly noted."

"And now that's out of the way, I'll take the Smart Home for $1 million, Alex."

"The Smart Home?"

"You know, like how people control their houses with their phones. An app adjusts the thermostat and tells you when to buy milk and knows what temperature you like your bath water—that sort of thing."

"Of course. Home technology is big now. Good thinking."

"You're welcome. Have a nice day. Bye!" she teased.

"Hey, you're not getting off that easy," he reeled her back in. "Aren't you curious why I'm asking?"

"I'm part curious, part nervous. After our Cherokee Park adventure last week, I'm not sure if I should ask."

"Good enough for me," he replied. "The thing is you were so good at pretending to be my wife I wondered if you would want to do it again."

"Oh brother," she groaned. "What's the angle this time?"

Cal could tell her apprehension was feigned. She was being coy, and he liked it.

"The good news is you get to play another multi-millionaire. This time we are entrepreneurial investors."

"Hmm. And the bad news?"

"We have to play the part in a crowded room full of actual rich people. Could be a little more challenging than last time. And there is more at stake."

"Well, you've managed to pique my curiosity. Where pray tell is the setting for this latest ruse?"

"Oh, just the Bonnycastle Gala. No big deal," Cal responded facetiously.

"Oh my. Why didn't you say so in the first place!"

"Does that mean you want to go?"

"I'm pretty sure I hate every person who ever attends that party, but I would love to see what happens at it."

"I'll mark you down as a yes then."

"Fine. So do you plan to give me a name this time or will I need to come up with it on the fly while the marks are staring me in the eye?" she joked.

Cal cringed at the reminder of his mistake.

"Our last name is Diamond. You pick the first."

"Oh, wow, real subtle!" she laughed. "I'm going with, let's see, Suzanne. Suzanne Diamond."

"Frank and Suzanne Diamond, it is. Has a nice ring to it I think."

"Sounds like a winner. Quick question: Do you ever go on normal dates? Dinner and a movie is starting to look pretty good about now."

"You know you like it," he retorted. "I'll pick you up about five on Saturday. By the way, the MG is fixed, in case you were wondering."

"Thank goodness. Alright. Well, I'll see you then!"

Cal was smiling when he hung up the phone. It was a good day so far. He decided to go for a drive.

The so-called distillery district of Lexington was an up-and-coming hot spot in the city where several new bars and restaurants had sprung up over the past few years. The area boasted a unique blend of hip style juxtaposed against decades of decaying buildings and overgrown greenery. Something about the graffiti and crumbling brick of dilapidated warehouses attracted the tastemakers of the Lexington social scene.

A recent revitalization effort had seen dozens of new murals painted across the distillery district's abandoned buildings, and the combination of an edgy artist vibe with gourmet food and eclectic cocktails drew a crowd of people from all different backgrounds. It was one of Cal's favorite new spots to grab a drink.

He cruised up Manchester Street with the top down, taking in the scene around him. He was headed for the center of the distillery district, a strip of breweries and restaurants sure to always have something exciting happening by mid-afternoon.

He glanced at his watch. About four o'clock. Maybe a little early for happy hour, but it's never stopped me before, Cal thought. Besides it's a beautiful day to sit outside with a drink. Patio weather.

Brake lights up ahead caused him to slow just before reaching his destination. As he approached the car in front of him, he realized there was a long line of traffic and no one was moving an inch. A complete standstill.

When his car came to a stop at the end of line, he raised up in his seat and peered over the windshield at the line of traffic. The brake lights stretched as far as he could see. Something serious must be going on up there. An accident?

He turned to look behind him and saw he had been penned in by more travelers. They, too, had confused looks on their faces, wondering why this usually open road was so congested. He made eye contact with the driver behind him and shrugged his shoulders.

Since no one was moving, he pulled the parking brake and got out. He walked toward the source of the commotion. As he got closer to the front of the line, he could hear honking horns and angry shouts from stranded motorists.

"Hey, buddy, who made you king of the traffic jam?" a man chided Cal as he walked by.

Cal ignored him and continued heading toward the source of the congestion.

As soon as he rounded a slight bend in the road, he realized what was happening. Halcott Industries was just ahead on the left and, like their home, the headquarters of the Halcott business was getting a healthy dose of PETA protests.

Police in riot gear lined the property of the large industrial building. Across the street, protestors were waving signs and hurling insults through bullhorns.

"STOP RACING HORSES TO THE GRAVE!" one group was chanting.

Another faction of the protest featured women dressed in dominatrix gear, complete with thigh-high leather boots and whips. The hands that didn't wield whips carried signs that read:

"YOU MIGHT LIKE WHIPS BUT HORSES DON'T!"

In yet another corner of the protest, people were crawling around on all fours with saddles on their backs. Some of them even had people riding the saddles as they crawled around the shoulder of the road.

The cars at the front of the traffic line were getting a real show. They honked their horns and cat-called the protestors, paying particular attention to the dominatrices.

"Wow," was all Cal could muster. He stood watching the scene in front of him.

"Ain't that some shit?"

Cal jumped as the guy in the car next to him spoke. He hadn't realized how close he was standing to the line of traffic.

"Yeah, really. I knew they did this, but it's the first time I have seen it," he replied. "How long have you been stopped here?"

Before the guy could answer, the commotion ahead grew to a crescendo. Police rushed from the post they held at the front doors of Halcott Industries. Cal followed their trajectory with his eyes and spotted the cause of the sudden change in energy.

A man wearing nothing but a plastic horse head was crisscrossing back and forth across the road.

"Streaker!" someone shouted and everyone in the cars began honking and cheering for the naked man as he evaded the grasp of police. Needless to say, the cops were trying to take him down with as little physical contact as possible.

Cal watched and smiled. The whole spectacle was mildly entertaining. The cops would approach, and the man would take off in another direction. His fellow PETA members cheered each time he evaded the grasp of the law. The naked man was like a dog being chased by its owner. He would wait until they were right near him and then he would take off again.

After a few minutes of the chase game, the police cornered the naked man and hemmed him in from behind. There was no escape when he turned to run this time, and they finally took him down.

The streaker was tackled and forced to lie face down, naked on the gravel with a knee in his back and cuffs on his wrists.

"That couldn't possibly be comfortable," Cal said to the guy in the car next to him.

The driver laughed and shook his head.

The first car in line used the opportunity to ease around the group of policemen who were attending to the arrest. The second car followed and before long, traffic was slowly crawling again.

Cal walked back to his own car and hopped in. When his turn came, he too crept around the protest, glancing again at the wild scene as he passed it.

18

The Fire Pit was Cal's regular joint in the distillery district. You never knew what kind of crowd would be there. He had seen bikers pull up in gangs and line the front wall with motorcycles. He had also seen a Keeneland crowd dressed to the nines in suits and sundresses pack the place after the day's last race. It was always a surprise what music would be cranking on the jukebox.

The bar was already filling up for a Wednesday. As expected, the Keeneland crowd was filtering in as the race day wound down. Cal grabbed a stool at the bar and ordered a beer.

Next to him, a trio of drinkers was discussing the PETA protest down the street.

"Hey, I don't care what you guys say. That dominatrix chick can use the whip on me anytime," one guy was saying. "Spare the rod, spoil the child, am I right?" he joked.

"You're sick in the head, man. Everything is a big joke to you clowns," the second guy responded. "How would you like it if some dude was riding you while you got hit with that whip? I support the protestors."

"Damn hippie," chimed in a third drinker. "Probably gonna tell us you're a vegetarian now, too. God, I hate vegetarians."

"What are you bitching about down there, Hank?" The first guy leaned forward and addressed the third speaker. "You're just mad cause every woman you've looked at lately has been sparing your rod."

The whole group laughed uproariously at that one, including Hank. He knew he had been gotten.

Cal smiled at the joke. He stared forward into the recesses of liquor bottles before him.

He was beginning to question his decision to include Emma in the Bonnycastle mansion plan. Especially with a potentially dangerous man like Gallo involved. Emma was an innocent bystander in this case. She wasn't even getting paid for her part in the investigation. Cal was afraid he might be taking advantage of her.

But this was not a one-sided affair. He liked her. And he wanted to spend time with her, so it wasn't like he was using her. Besides, she was obviously excited about attending an exclusive party renowned for its rich and famous guest list.

For that matter, Emma had proven herself to be tough and smart. She certainly wasn't helpless, and she did not need to be tended to like a child. She was a strong woman and had already acted as a valuable asset to his investigation. Frankly, he needed her. Either way, he resolved to be cautious because the last thing he wanted was for anyone to get hurt as a result of carelessness.

Cal sensed a presence to his right. The open bar stool had been occupied.

"Took a while to track you down, but I finally found you," came a gruff voice from the newly occupied seat.

Cal turned to see who was addressing him. It was Jubal Early! A rush of panic shot through Cal's veins. He did his best not to betray any surprise. He nodded at Early and smiled. Play dumb.

"Hello there, old boy! What brings you to Lexington?" he replied in his best impersonation of the accent he had previously affected.

"Cut the shit. I know exactly who you are and what you do, Tyson," was Early's curt response. "Now why don't you tell me what the hell is really going on."

Early's demeanor made it clear to Cal the gig was up. And he really didn't have any reason to maintain the schtick. Early was a weirdo, but he was probably clear. Might as well be honest. Cal dropped the accent and came clean.

"Look, there's no reason for me to lie anymore. I assume you know I am investigating the Halcott death."

"That's the word on the street. Once I learned you were a private investigator, the pieces all came together."

"As a man who has spent a lot of time tracking people who don't want to be found, I have to admire your accomplishment," Cal acknowledged. "How did you do it, anyway?"

"Your little lady's license plate was the giveaway. She was something else, I might add. Had me blinded during our meeting."

Cal sank inside. A crucial oversight. They were pretending to be from Bowling Green but driving a car with Fayette County plates. Dumb. He remembered now how Early had stared at the car as they drove away from the diner.

"Well done. So you got us. Guess I should apologize for leading you on about the possibility of work."

"Whatever. I probably wouldn't have accepted your offer anyway. You came off as a naive amateur. I'm over it."

That stung a little. Cal winced.

"Fair enough," he replied through clenched teeth. "Did you drive all the way to Lexington to call me out, or do you have something else to say?" Cal was already getting tired of Early and was ready to escape the situation.

Early was unfazed. He was used to dealing with people he didn't like.

"You asked me about Augusto Gallo. Are you going after him?"

"Maybe. Why?" Cal was making no effort to pacify Early anymore.

"Because if you are, I want to help," Early retorted. "He's a nasty guy and he has pissed me off more times than I can count. I know a lot more about him than I let on during our first conversation. Between you and me, I wouldn't be surprised at all to learn he arranged a murder."

Cal's ears perked up at this news. Maybe Early was worth talking to after all.

"OK, I'm listening."

The bar was filling up around them. Cal kept getting jostled in the back by a guy attempting to order drinks for he and his date.

"Two Jack and Cokes!" the guy was shouting as he waved a $20 in the air.

The bartender was deliberately avoiding him. Cal didn't blame her, but he really wanted to get this asshole off his back. He leaned over to Early. "Can we take this outside?"

Early grunted and stood up. Cal followed his lead and threw a subtle elbow at the prick behind him as he edged past.

Once outside, Early headed for the namesake of the bar, where a bonfire burned in an outdoor fire pit year-round. He chose an empty corner of the patio and turned to face the fire. Cal joined him and waited for Early to continue talking.

The sun was just beginning its downward trajectory toward the tree line surrounding the fire pit. Cicadas croaked and hummed all around them. The chirping sound mixed with the chatter of small groups on the patio created an ambient din that enveloped Cal and Early in a shroud of privacy. They could talk freely without fear of eavesdroppers.

"Like I was saying, Gallo has a lot of secrets and I believe the horse racing industry would be better off without him in it," Early spoke into the fire. "If I can help make that happen, I'm willing to try."

Cal felt a little guilty for his shortness with Early. He softened up and coaxed him for more information.

"I would be lying if I said I had Gallo pegged. To be honest, I'm not even sure how I am going to start a conversation with him."

"I can't help you there. Let's just say Gallo and I are not on friendly terms."

"Point taken. What else can you tell me about him?"

"He has no moral compass. I might be an asshole, but I do have a code of conduct. I know what I believe in and you can trust I'll be consistent about it."

Cal was worried Early might launch into another state's rights rant. He focused the conversation.

"What did Gallo do to you?"

"The general public has no idea how much bullshit happens off track in the stables. It can get pretty bad."

Cal remained silent.

"I saw the PETA protest on my way here. I was a few cars behind you."

Early let that announcement sink in for a second. Cal made no move to interrupt him. Both men stared into the burning flames. Smoke swayed before them like a Middle Eastern belly dancer. Mesmerizing, drawing them in and then lashing them with a wave of choking heat that singed their nostrils and forced them to squint their eyes in submission.

Early continued, "Whips are nothing compared to the shit some of those guys pump into their horses."

"Drugs you mean?"

"You could say that. But maybe not the kind of drugs you'd think." Early paused. He glanced around and nervously looked over his shoulder. Lowering his voice, he proceeded.

"Sure, they inject them with speed and other performance-enhancing crap. And, as you might guess, there's no shortage of painkillers either.

Cal nodded.

"But what you might not expect is the amount of *performance-decreasing* drugs lurking around in the stables."

"Decreasing? Why?" Cal was surprised.

"You've heard of boxers throwing a fight? Well, horses don't work like that. You can't tell a thoroughbred not to run. It's in his blood. He loves to run. He's made to run. People don't realize how competitive racehorses are. When they break from the post, they come out with everything they've got. I don't care what anyone says, a racehorse wants to win, and it will try for the victory no matter what the owner wants."

"Interesting," Cal mused.

"Yeah. A boxer, you give him a portion of the jack and he'll take a dive in the third. Whatever you want, the price is right, you got it from a boxer. Not from a horse. A horse you've got to find some other way to make him lose if you got money on it. A horse don't give up."

"I had no idea." Cal was shocked at this insider's confession. "Do you mean to say Gallo manipulates race results by drugging horses to make them lose?"

"I mean to say just that."

Cal whistled softly to show his surprise.

"We must have butted heads a dozen times while I worked for the Halcotts because Gallo tried to get me to drug our horses and other horses waiting to race in the track stables."

"But you never did it?"

Early looked perturbed. "You got something in your ears, boy? I told you I have a code of ethics and I don't break it for anyone. I told Gallo to shove that syringe up his ass."

This struck Cal as funny, but Early remained stone-faced.

Cal pushed for more. "So that got you on Gallo's bad side?"

"You better believe it. I got death threats. Actual death threats. I'm positive they came from his goons. He never tried anything, but either way that will scare a man."

"No doubt."

Cal paused to consider this new information. Both men stared at the fire burning in front of them.

After a few moments, Cal spoke again.

"Let me ask you this—have you ever run into a guy with a nasty scar across his eye?"

Early thought for a minute. "No, can't say I have. Why?"

"Just a theory," Cal replied and changed the subject. "I'm actually planning to meet Gallo this weekend at the Bonnycastle Gala."

"Whoa, that's some high roller stuff right there. Do you think you'll actually get close enough to poke around?"

"Everyone keeps asking me that. It's starting to make me worry," Cal replied. "But I am certainly going to try." Then he had another thought. "Do you ever go to that party?"

Early looked at him like Cal had just proposed marriage.

"You've got to be out of your damn mind if you think I'd go to a party like that, even if I was invited. No chance in hell."

"Hey, I didn't want to make any assumptions."

Cal slid his notebook from his back pocket and flipped through it to see if he was missing anything. He spotted a note that reminded him of a lingering question.

"I wanted to ask you this the other day, but I wasn't sure how to bring it up. Guess it doesn't matter now." Cal continued, "I saw a photograph in the March 25th issue of the *Courier-Journal* with you standing next to the Halcotts and their horse Valkyrie. It confused me because hadn't you already severed ties at that point?"

Early shrugged the question off.

"Yeah, I remember that. Sterling was all about maintaining appearances in the public eye. He constantly worried a scandal would blight his image. And this year he was particularly concerned about any negative publicity surrounding his Derby bid."

"Sure, I get it."

"Anyhow, he knew how to take advantage of a photo op. It was totally random I happened to be at Churchill Downs that day. I was working out some other horses early that morning. On my way out of the stables, Halcott called me over. Next thing I knew, I was posing in photos for the newspaper."

Cal listened quietly. Early's story seemed too perfect somehow. It didn't quite add up.

"I thought you guys didn't get along?"

"We don't, but what the hell do I care? He stuffed a handful of bills in my shirt pocket after it was over at least."

The explanation sounded fishy, but it seemed to check out.

Cal was ready to wrap things up. Before leaving, he had one more idea.

"Would you be willing to testify against Gallo in court if the opportunity ever presented itself?"

"I don't know, man. I've never been a rat. I don't like that idea. I'll have to think about it."

Early seemed to be turning the idea over in his head before continuing.

"Course it won't matter if he gets to you first. I'm telling you; he will not give up easily. You better watch your back."

Cal nodded. He could tell Early was serious.

"For what it's worth I do hope you get that prick. I believe he's your man." Early reached into his back pocket and extracted a business card, which he handed to Cal. "Give me a call if I can help anymore."

And with that, Early left the fire circle and headed for the gravel parking lot.

The fire popped loudly as a log shifted in the heat and fell into the glowing pit of embers.

19

The rest of the week passed without incident, and finally Saturday arrived. The Derby was exactly one week away, and the festivities would begin tonight in Louisville. The Bonnycastle Gala kicked it all off.

Cal was feeling a little nervous throughout the afternoon as he showered, shaved, and donned the tuxedo he kept in the back of his closet for events like this one. It wasn't often he pulled the tux out of its garment bag, but over the years, the purchase had paid off.

No one shows up to a party like the Bonnycastle in a rented tuxedo. People at this level notice details like that and an ill-fitting suit could blow his cover. Cal was glad he had taken the time to get his suit tailored to the cut of his body. Although he rarely wore the tux, it felt good as he pulled it on again. He glanced in the full-length mirror on the back of his closet door. Looks good, if I do say so myself.

But feeling good in a tux in one's house and feeling good in a room full of people who wear tuxes every weekend are two totally different things. Cal knew he would have to play his part well tonight if he wanted to avoid suspicion. If the crowd sensed weakness, they would eat him alive.

He wasn't worried about committing a social faux pas; he simply knew, if he wanted to have any chance of getting close to Gallo, he would need to nail his character and work every angle.

He had constructed a plan to get Gallo talking and it involved the entrepreneurial investment idea he and Emma had come up with. His research on Gallo indicated he had a penchant for gambling in the startup community, and Cal had resolved to pitch Gallo an ownership stake in his new Smart Home business as an entry point for the conversation.

As he fashioned his bowtie, he thought about Emma. The guilty thoughts were creeping back again. Was he doing the right thing to bring her along? What if he embarrassed her? Or worse…

He shook the thoughts from his mind. This is happening. Let's make the most of it. They might even have a little fun. He had not talked to her since Wednesday, and he was looking forward to seeing her again. He wondered what she was wearing.

Then another thought entered his consciousness. Harper had given him a hard time on the phone when he mentioned bringing a date. Was she going to make this weird? He knew for a fact Emma was not Harper's biggest fan. That dynamic could get tricky.

His phone buzzed on the dresser to his left. He stepped away from the mirror and checked to see who had messaged him.

Ear rings: pearls or diamonds?

Cal smiled. He knew better than to take a stand on a date's fashion sense—especially at an event like the one tonight.

You're going to look amazing in either.

He placed the phone on his desk and sat down to give his shoes a quick once-over to remove any remaining scuffs. The phone buzzed again.

What a copout. Wimp.
Hey, I know better. Which are you going with?
Oh, you'll just have to wait and see I guess…
Fine. I see how you are. Be there in about 30 minutes? Don't forget to grab the rings.
Yes, dear. See you then!

Cal slid the phone into his pocket and pulled on his shoes. He was ready. He stood up and fixed his bowtie in the mirror.

"Let's do this," he said to his reflection.

Cal grabbed his keys and headed for the front door, but as he reached for the knob, he instead heard a knock come from the other side.

He froze and then took two slow steps back from the door. Given the circumstances of the evening, he was apprehensive about receiving unexpected guests.

"Yes. Who's there?" he asked through the closed door.

"Special delivery for a Mr. Cal Tyson," was the response from the other side.

Cal wasn't taking any chances. He placed his right foot on the chair by the door and slid up his pant leg, exposing a concealed holster from which he drew his .38. He raised the weapon to his chest and quietly cocked it.

"Just a second."

He took a detour to the dining room and carefully pulled the curtain away from the window, which gave him a clear view of his front porch.

At the door was a man dressed in a chauffeur's suit and hat. He stood stiffly, back straight, gloved hands at his side.

Cal's mind began to race. He certainly had not hired a chauffeur. Could this be another hitman sent by John Hood? What if Gallo himself had learned Cal was investigating him and wanted to stop the case before it even begins. There were a lot of variables at play and it was nearly impossible to guess the motive of the man standing on his front porch.

He watched the chauffeur raise his hand and knock on the door again.

"Excuse me, sir, we really must be going if we are to arrive on time," came the muffled voice through the door.

Cal relaxed, and his curiosity took over.

"If anyone is coming for me, they probably aren't likely to make a move in broad daylight on my front porch," he spoke under his breath. "I'm sure it's fine."

He returned to the door and pulled it open, keeping the .38 behind his back.

"Hello, I'm Cal. How can I help you?"

"Good afternoon, sir. I've been sent by Ms. Harper Halcott. She wishes me to escort you and your guest to the party tonight."

As he spoke, he stepped aside and waved his arm to the street where there was parked a jet black, freshly waxed limousine.

Cal immediately loosened up. He swung the door open and laughed. As he did so, he placed the .38 on an end table near the door.

"Of course. Come in. Wow, that is certainly unexpected," he said to the chauffeur.

"Madam has requested I deliver to you this note, as well."

The driver proffered a white envelope emblazoned with the name:

M. Tyson

Cal took the envelope and slid his finger along the seal. He opened it and extracted the thick note card inside.

Dear Mr. Tyson,

I could not possibly let you arrive as my guest in that dreadful convertible. What would people think?

Please accept this driver as a gift in exchange for your ongoing commitment to our arrangement. I cannot thank you enough for what you have done so far, and I look forward to what I can only hope will be your eventual resolution.

See you tonight.

Truly,
Harper

"She never ceases to surprise me," was all Cal could say to the chauffeur. "Give me a second and I will be right out."

"Very good, sir."

The driver returned to the limousine and waited patiently at the back door of the vehicle.

Cal slid on his tuxedo coat and returned the .38 to its ankle holster. He dropped Harper's card on the table and stepped through the door into the late April afternoon.

When the driver saw Cal exit the house, he pulled open the back door of the limo. Cal climbed in and watched as the door was shut behind him.

Little did Cal know, one of the craziest nights of his life had just begun.

20

Emma answered her door to find their chauffeur waiting on her porch. Cal remained in the vehicle and watched through the tinted back window as her expression went from confused to excited. He couldn't hear the conversation, but it was clear Emma was impressed.

She raised her chin to peer over the driver's shoulder and shook her head at the car's darkened back window. Her mouth expanded into a grin and she waved.

Cal coolly lowered the window to get a better look at his date. He had to focus in order to keep his emotions in check as he stared up at Emma. She was ravishing.

He knew she was pretty, but tonight her beauty had reached a new level. Her long, silky black gown fit snugly against her supple frame. It flowed smoothly around her as she stepped down the front stairs. She wore long white gloves that stretched to her elbows. Retro style, reminiscent of a 1960s movie star.

The ensemble was capped off with a simple string of pearls around her neck and a pearl in each ear. Her eyes were covered by large round sunglasses that perfectly matched the era to which her white gloves hearkened.

The driver reached the back door first and pulled it open, stepping aside and bowing for Emma to enter. Cal had not taken his eyes off of her.

"I didn't realize I was dating Grace Kelly. You look incredible," was all the greeting he could muster.

She smiled and snickered softly.

"Thank you. The tux makes you look dashing. If I'm Grace Kelly, then you are James Bond."

"My friends call me 007. Now get in here and let me take you in."

He grabbed her wrist and pulled her carefully into the backseat. The driver shut the door and walked around to the front. As he did, Cal swept Emma close to his body and kissed her deeply. After a few seconds, he opened his eyes with their lips still touching and breathed quietly into her mouth.

"This is going to be a good night," he said as the limousine pulled away from the curb.

If the driver was listening carefully on the way to Louisville, he would have heard giggling and low voices coming from the back seat. Then, he might have heard rapid breathing, followed by sighs, and then the pop of a champagne bottle somewhere around Exit 30.

But the driver was a modest man. He kept to his own affairs and therefore heard nothing more than the classical music emanating from the car's radio, accompanied by the tapping of his own thumbs on the leather steering wheel.

In the back seat of the limousine, Cal was pouring Dom Pérignon into two champagne flutes. Emma lounged and extended her hand to accept the glass Cal was passing her.

Both of their faces were flushed, and Cal's bowtie was slightly askew. Emma took a sip from the champagne and leaned forward to fix Cal's tie. As she neared his face, Cal stole another kiss and then sipped from his own glass.

"Harper sure knows how to make us feel welcome," he said as he raised his glass in a toast. "To the woman who made this possible."

Emma smiled, but she was visibly put off by the untimely reference.

"Indeed, but I could have done without hearing her name at this particular moment!"

Cal realized his mistake and apologized.

"That's okay, you rascal. Now put on your wedding band."

She removed the rings from her clutch and handed one to Cal. He accepted the ring quietly and slid it over his finger.

"Seriously, I can't believe she got us a limo!" Emma broke the silence. "We are really going to arrive in style."

The driver signaled a right turn to take the Grinstead exit off of I-64. They were only a few miles away now.

Cal's stomach tightened with nerves. He glanced over at Emma. She seemed perfectly at ease and comfortable. It was as though she came to the Bonnycastle Mansion every year.

At least one of us is prepared for this, he thought.

The car rambled along the highway, curving through historic streets as it approached The Highlands neighborhood. The landscape grew denser with trees that hid the surrounding city. Giant oak, maple, poplar, elm trees hundreds of years old blotted out the city lights. Cherokee Park was a private island sheltered from the bustle of town.

Out the window, Cal watched as the landscape changed into the secluded stretch of Louisville reserved for the exclusive, the rich and famous. The driveways were so long he could barely see the mansions sitting atop the hills. The elaborate vistas could just as easily be those of the Hollywood Hills in Los Angeles. The area they were entering was not often seen by eyes like his.

The night was crisp, but not cold. The light scent of spring flowers poked through the dry air as winter receded, banishing the earthy musk of unraked leaves to the loam of years past.

They rounded a bend and saw, perched high atop a hill, the Bonnycastle Mansion in all its glory. The mansion sat directly across from Cherokee Park, where Cal and Emma had been walking just two weeks before. But today they were in a private corner of the park where the public is not allowed to venture without express invitation from one of the neighboring landowners.

The vista across the street darkened as the sun slid below the horizon. The heavily wooded landscape created the illusion they were in a lost, remote location. Trees walled off views on all sides, hiding the lights of downtown and hemming in the inhabitants of the private gala. Despite being in the middle of the city, it felt as though they could be miles from civilization.

Shadows from the surrounding trees stretched long as the last light of day disappeared completely and washed the mansion and its inhabitants in a shroud of blackness.

The long driveway was lined by ornate lights partially buried every three feet the whole way up to the house. The lights gave the entrance a sort of runway-like quality, as though each vehicle may land and take off without ever needing to touch down on the surrounding streets.

At the end of the runway, the mansion was lit up like a stage. There could be no mistaking the site of the party. The house was glowing like an alien spaceship, ready to blast off and transport the guests to another galaxy.

It was just after 8:00 p.m. when their limousine turned into the driveway and fell in line behind the long stretch of vehicles bearing the party's early V.I.P.s. The guests arrived in impressive fashion. Lamborghinis, Maseratis, Bentleys, Aston Martins. Every car Cal had ever dreamed of, but never seen in person.

One celebrity after the next climbed out of these magnificent machines and handed their keys to waiting valets. Cal couldn't decide if a valet gig here would be great or terrifying.

As they edged toward the house, the scene began to take shape.

The front yard was full of revelers milling about in preparation for what they all knew was one of the top ten annual parties in the world. White-clad waiters carried trays full of champagne glasses and hors d'œuvres from one group to the next. The party guests casually grabbed full glasses and surrendered their empties mid-conversation without missing a beat. It takes practice to execute a maneuver like that so fluidly.

Cal and Emma watched the festivities out the window as they waited to join them. They couldn't hear anything, but the reserved laughter and witty banter needed no subtitles.

Finally, it was their turn to exit the limo and step into the crowd of people. The driveway was lined with paparazzi, and camera bulbs were flashing all around the vehicle.

The chauffeur stepped out and walked around to the backseat to open the door. Cal could see through the heavily tinted windows they were surrounded by photographers.

"They are in for a disappointment I'm afraid," he said as the door opened, and the melee began.

Two dozen flashes went off instantly as the door opened. Cal slid out first and turned to help Emma step from the car. He blocked the view of the photographers with his body to allow her some privacy as she exited the limousine.

A thick red carpet had been laid out at the front entryway of the house where everyone was being dropped. The paparazzi swarmed the edges of it. They pressed against each other and shouted the names of the celebrities on parade, hoping to get an elusive photo for which the tabloids would pay a year's salary.

As soon as Cal and Emma had both landed firmly on the carpet, a groan of disappointment passed through the group of photographers.

"Who are they?" someone shouted.

"Who cares!" answered another.

And, as quickly as they had begun, the sea of flashes receded like low tide at the beach.

Some of the amateur photographers continued snapping shots just in case Cal and Emma were lesser known wealthy celebrities whose photographs might fetch a few hundred bucks in a small tabloid. But most of them lowered their cameras and saved their energy for the next drop off.

Cal and Emma found their footing and started walking up the carpet toward the front door of the mansion.

"Ooh, is that Paris Hilton?!" screeched a paparazzo behind them.

"I don't know, but I heard a rumor she was coming tonight!"

And with that, the cameras rushed to face the next limousine in line.

Cal and Emma didn't care in the least. They were doing their best to enjoy this brief brush with celebrity without getting completely overwhelmed by it.

Emma leaned into Cal's ear as they split the line of photographers. "Did they get your good side?"

He smiled and turned his head toward her. She was still sporting her Grace Kelly sunglasses. The dark lenses hid her eyes, but they were sparkling under the shades.

"How did I get so lucky?" he asked.

She raised her chin and adopted a pose of mock arrogance, and then pranced into the house, clutching Cal's arm the entire way.

As soon as they stepped inside, the real celebrity-spotting began.

"Oh my god. Don't look now, but Hugh Hefner is in the corner surrounded by his bunnies."

Cal casually followed Emma's eyes until he spotted the Playboy baron. He had a 22-year-old bombshell on each arm and was chatting with a group of couples near a gigantic, floor-to-ceiling stone fireplace.

"What a life," Cal teased. The joke was met with a slap on the forearm from his date.

"Behave yourself and focus. Now do you see Gallo in here?"

Cal scanned the room. He saw more rock stars and celebrities than he could possibly count, but no sign of Gallo yet. He shook his head.

"Not yet. From what I understand, crowds are not really his scene. Maybe he is in one of these side rooms." As he spoke, Cal surveyed the layout of the house. There were halls everywhere that led down dark passageways. He could hear muffled conversations coming from every direction. No telling what all is happening here tonight.

Emma sensed his thoughts. She, too, was trying to take in the expansive architecture of the mansion.

"I wouldn't be a bit surprised if there is some crazy *Eyes Wide Shut* action happening behind one of those closed doors," she whispered.

"Just remember the secret password."

"I'd rather not. Let's get a drink."

They hit a makeshift bar set up against one wall of the house's crowded great room. The bartender behind it wore a caterer's tux. His hair was slicked on the sides and tied up in a bun in back. He wore a heavy stubble and an earring in each ear.

"What can I pour for you?" he asked as they approached the bar.

"Ginger ale for me and…" he turned to look at Emma, waiting for her to place an order.

"Vodka tonic with a twist."

"…and a vodka tonic with a twist for the lady," Cal shifted back to the bartender and finished his request.

Emma wasn't satisfied with Cal's order.

"Oh, come on, old man. This is a party. At least have *one* with me," she goaded.

Cal relented. He wanted a drink pretty badly anyway. He desperately needed to loosen up and take the edge off.

"I'll go with a splash of Wild Turkey."

"80 or 101?"

"Uh, 101. Just a splash, though."

What am I doing? This is probably a bad idea. But Cal shook off the thought. He took his glass from the bar and touched it to Emma's.

The tartness from the lemon rind that had encircled Emma's glass wafted through the air between them. The scent was fresh and clean. It opened their capillaries and lightened the mood.

"To a good night with good company."

"And to not getting murdered by thugs," Emma added.

"That, too."

They raised their glasses and drank.

The bartender had a perplexed look on his face when Cal turned back to him.

"Oh, um, just a little joke we have at big parties like this," he attempted to assuage the bartender's concerns. Then he changed the subject. "So this is nice and all, but I was kind of expecting a bigger crowd."

"First timers, eh?" the bartender asked. "You haven't been out back yet."

"Aha."

Cal winked at Emma and they both headed for the back door. He couldn't help nodding at Hef on his way past the fireplace. He turned to see if Emma had noticed. Her eyes were fixed on the exit.

They reached the threshold of the mansion's back door with drinks in hand and prepared to enter the heart of the soiree. They paused at the door to take it all in.

What they saw was beyond anything either had ever imagined. It was completely surreal. It was like a movie and they were about to step through the screen.

"Now this is a party," Emma mouthed, and they advanced through the aperture into the silver screen before them.

21

The backyard of the Bonnycastle Mansion was packed with hundreds of people, all dressed in black ties and evening gowns. The patio was abuzz with conversation and the sound of clinking glasses.

In a corner of the yard near the garden, a stage had been constructed. On it, a jazz band was carrying the party's soundtrack over the din of the lively crowd. Saxophone, trumpet, piano, stand-up bass, drum kit. The music was subtle but lively. A few of the partygoers were nodding their heads to the rhythm, occasionally turning to glance toward the stage in appreciation of a poignant solo.

Strings of festive lights hung from lattice work that surrounded the entire yard. They crisscrossed the patio above the heads of the crowd and emitted a dim luminescence that gave the party a cozy feeling. It was bright enough to see the old-fashioned brick patio beneath their feet, but dark enough to obscure the faces in the crowd.

From Cal's vantage point, the lighting created an effect that made the entire backyard appear blended, a hazy wave of definitionless shapes that faded into each other, one after the next, leading from the stairs on which he stood all the way to the stage about 100 yards in the distance.

"Frankie! Yoo-hoo! Earth to Frank!"

Cal was mesmerized by the scene in front of him and had missed the voice repeatedly calling out the name of his alias. He snapped out of it and turned his head in the direction of the voice.

It was Harper, of course. She was standing at the bottom of the stairs among a group of debonair actor types and waving up at Cal. When his eyes finally focused, he smiled and headed down the stairs to greet her.

"Hello there, Ms. Halcott," he spoke as he approached the group.

She leaned forward and breathed, "You ass. Don't ever make me look stupid like that again. You are still going with the name, right?"

Harper's familiar lavender scent enveloped him as powerfully as did her physical embrace. It made the hair on his neck tingle. He experienced the fragrance with all of his senses. In the flash of a second the scent rushed through his blood to his brain and his toes and everywhere in between. Almost like a momentary paralysis. Cal wondered if rich people have secret access to exclusive perfumes not available to the general public because whatever Harper wore was inescapably powerful.

He attempted to speak. To apologize. To greet her. Anything. But before he could respond, she had turned to the group and presented his introduction.

"Excuse me, everyone. Allow me to introduce Mr. Frank Diamond. He is an entrepreneur from Lexington."

She turned her gaze to focus on one man in the group and addressed him directly.

"Stephen, maybe you can convince Mr. Diamond to invest in one of your inventions."

She laughed and returned to Cal.

"Frankie, you absolutely must meet Stephen. He has made several advancements in the thoroughbred industry. I just know the two of you will hit it off," she drawled. "You are always looking for new technology, are you not?"

Cal nodded and started to answer, but she immediately cut him off again. Harper was in rare form tonight.

"And, Frankie, who do we have here? I heard a rumor you settled down. This must be your bride."

She parted the crowd and waved Emma over.

"Join the circle, dear, and introduce yourself. Let us have a look at you."

And with that, she grabbed Emma's wrist and thrust her into the center of the group, giving her a spin for the audience.

Cal could see Emma was stunned. He was caught off guard himself.

"Uh, yes, um, this is my wife Suzanne," he stammered.

Harper didn't miss a beat. "Charmed, I'm sure. So lovely to finally meet you, dear. Welcome to the party."

She regripped Emma's hand and withdrew her from center stage to the outskirts of the party, where she began to grill her more privately.

Cal could hear the conversation proceed between the two women to his right.

"What do you think of the mansion?" Harper was saying. "Your glass is empty, dear. We must get you a refill. Come with me and we will take a tour."

Cal caught Emma's eyes as she was dragged away. She tilted her head as if to say, "here goes nothing," and then she gave into Harper's will and vanished into the crowd.

The rest of the group had recovered from Harper's animated introduction. They resumed the conversations they were having prior to the interruption.

Cal stood on the outskirts of the group and listened. It didn't take long before he heard a voice on his left.

"So you invest in startups, eh?"

It was the man who Harper had introduced as Stephen. By now, Cal had gathered his thoughts. He was ready to assume his character for the evening.

"If the ROI is right, yes, I do. I am a businessman first, of course, and I love to make money. But that being said, I enjoy investing in local businesses when I see they have promise," Cal launched into the corporate lingo he knew the situation called for. "So what kind of advancements have you made in horse racing? I'm a tech man myself actually."

"Well, not horse racing per se, but the thoroughbred industry in general. More like horse farms, I guess."

Cal listened and nodded. Stephen continued.

"If you have spent any time around these horse people, you know how crazy they can get about their animals. There is practically no limit to the budget when it comes to protecting their favorite thoroughbreds."

"Hmm…I like the direction this is heading."

"Exactly. So, anyhow, I created a custom, climate-controlled HVAC unit that mounts directly in the horse's stable. Each racehorse can adjust the temperature of its own stall anytime."

"You are kidding me. Are you telling me the horse actually sets a thermostat?"

"I know it sounds crazy, but yes. We have hoof controls embedded in the stall floor and we also mount a lever on the wall the horse can activate by nibbling."

Cal was laughing. "Forgive me, but I find that hilarious. I am imagining a horse's mane blowing in the wind of an air conditioner."

Stephen smiled along with him but remained serious. "Hey, if the business wasn't making me rich, I would be laughing too. It is admittedly pretty absurd. But I got over it quickly when I made my first million."

"You don't say? So there is a real market for this technology then?"

"I can't even keep up with the demand. I have a warehouse in Frankfort with three installation crews and I am having to turn clients away. We are booked through the end of the summer already."

"Fantastic. So you are looking for an investment to cashflow your expansion? Or was Harper just being dramatic?"

"To be honest, I hadn't given it much thought, but I may be open to a strategic partnership. A cash infusion would be nice, but at this point, I'm really more interested in a partner who wants to grow with the business."

Cal was getting caught up in the discussion. He was having fun. He was beginning to get lost in the character of Frank Diamond. Aside from personal interest, there was no reason to continue this conversation, but he was enjoying the role, so he kept it up.

"Funny you should say that because I might have something interesting to offer your business model."

Stephen was all ears.

"My portfolio is currently focused on Smart Home technology. You know, like using apps to control variables in our houses."

"Yeah?"

"Yeah. For example, we are developing an app that allows homeowners to control a thermostat."

Stephen suddenly got the connection and his face lit up.

"Now that *is* interesting. How hard would it be to adapt that technology to my climate-controlled stables?"

"Not hard at all. We would just need to give the units an internet connection. We would assign them a private IP address. From there, the app could access the hardware remotely and report back analytics or even take over control of the thermostat."

What in God's name am I doing, Cal thought. Stop this right now before you get in too deep.

He had just about exhausted his layman's knowledge of computer networking technology. One more probing question from Stephen and Cal would be exposed as a fraud.

But it was already too late. Stephen looked like a kid in a candy store. He wanted to know more.

"Wow. This is amazing. Could you foresee a possible relationship between our businesses?"

Cal started scrambling for an exit strategy. "Uh, it's certainly possible. Sounds like we have some overlapping interests…"

Cal lifted his eyes over Stephen's shoulder to scan around the crowded party. He was searching for Harper and Emma to extricate him from the mess he had created.

"Well, could we set up a meeting next week sometime? You are in Lexington, correct? I'm right down the road in Frankfort."

"Next week I will be out of town, but maybe the week after. Do you have a card on you?"

Stephen reached for his inner jacket pocket and withdrew a business card, which he handed to Cal.

Stephen Zipper
Proprietor,
Stability Solutions
"We stabilize your stable."

"That's me. My friends call me Zip. I would love to get together and talk more when you are free. This is so weird—I don't usually do this."

"Me neither," Cal replied, his statement carrying a lot more nuance than did Zip's. What now? He began to awkwardly withdraw from the circle of people.

Right on cue, Harper and Emma returned to the group and broke the uncomfortable silence. They were laughing and appeared to be having fun. Cal could tell they had imbibed a few more drinks on their excursion. Emma took his arm and smiled up at him. Her eyes had a slight glaze, and she looked happy.

"Hi there," Cal said.

"Hi."

"Well, I certainly hope you boys didn't talk business the entire time we were gone!" Harper interjected. "This is a party after all. Let's please have some fun!"

Emma took advantage of the outburst to lean into Cal's ear and whisper, "We need to talk."

22

The return of Harper and Emma provided enough of a distraction for Cal to step away from the circle. As he did, Emma slowly followed until the two were out of earshot of the rest of the group.

"What did you ladies do?"

"I think we're friends. I got a tour of the house. It is an amazing place, but never mind that now. I saw Gallo!"

"What? How? Where?" Cal couldn't decide which question to ask first.

"He's in the library at the end of that long hallway off the great room," Emma exclaimed. When I told Harper I am a librarian, she immediately dragged me to the library to show it off. As soon as we pushed open the door, we realized we had made a mistake."

"Really? What did you see?"

"There was a group of men. I didn't recognize any of them. They seemed important. Very well-dressed and slick-looking."

"And one of them was Gallo?"

"Apparently. I'm not entirely sure what he looks like, but Harper told me it was him after we closed the door."

"What were they talking about? Did you stay long?"

"No. As soon as we opened the door and stepped in, everything got silent. The men all stopped talking and turned toward us. It was obvious we were not welcome."

"You didn't hear anything?"

"Not really. I'm telling you, the second they saw us they stopped talking. One of them greeted Harper, but that was it."

"Can you get us back there?"

"I think so. Follow me."

They reentered the house and Emma headed straight for the hallway. The mansion was getting packed as the night wore on, and Cal had to squeeze in between people to maneuver through the room. Emma's lithe frame easily navigated the crowd, but Cal kept getting caught behind people. He was struggling to keep up.

"Excuse me, pal," a man said over his shoulder after Cal accidentally nudged him in the back. Cal turned and apologized.

"Sorry about that. Wild party, eh?"

The guy squinted his eyes and nodded. Cal immediately realized the shoulder he had just bumped belonged to Bono. Like, the Bono. He kept following Emma.

When they had successfully navigated the crowd, he caught her arm and said, "I'm pretty sure I just made Bono spill his drink."

148

"Check that off the bucket list," she responded as though she rubbed elbows with members of U2 every day. "Come on. The library is back here."

He followed her down the hallway until she stopped at a closed door and pointed. She mouthed the words, "This is it."

Cal put his ear to the door. He could hear muffled voices. The group of men were still inside. He strained to listen to the conversation, but he couldn't make out any words through the thick wooden door.

"Can you hear anything?"

"No."

Cal quietly turned the knobs of the adjacent doors. The first was locked, but the second swung open.

He reached his hand into the room and searched the walls for a light switch. He found it and flooded the room with yellow light. A bathroom. He entered, waved Emma in, and shut the door silently behind them.

"Wow, I could *live* in the bathroom at this freaking place," Emma whispered as she surveyed the new setting.

The bathroom was the size of a master bedroom. The place was tiled floor-to-ceiling with an intricate mosaic of cut marble. In the center of the room was a huge, porcelain soaking tub.

Cal scanned the bathroom wall shared with the library until his eyes rested on an antique ventilation duct near the ceiling above the toilet. The duct cover was brushed brass with a patina that probably predated the Civil War.

He walked across the room and climbed up on the toilet seat. He stretched for the vent, but still couldn't reach the duct cover. He steadied himself and stepped up to the tank behind the toilet.

Emma watched nervously as Cal slowly stood to his full height on the tank. His knees shook slightly as he extended them, causing the tank cover to rattle in place.

The higher step gave Cal exactly the height he needed. He reached the vent cover and removed it from the wall. He pressed his head against the tile, allowing his right ear to enter the ventilation duct inside the wall.

"Anything?" Emma stared up at him and whispered her question.

Cal held up his index finger in response to indicate he could hear something but needed silence to make out the words. He strained to listen to the voices in the next room.

"...have to keep this up for one more week," a voice was saying.

"You have no choice. It will all be worth it in the end. You know what the payout will be if he goes off at 50-1 and wins."

"He's right," came a third voice. "We only need to hang in there for a few more days and it will all be worth it. Right, Señor Gallo?"

"Yes. This is not up for discussion," came a voice with a thick Spanish accent. "We will do whatever it takes to protect our interests."

That must be Gallo, Cal thought.

Before he could relay his discovery to Emma, Cal heard a shout directly on the other side of the wall followed by a loud commotion. It sounded like a chair getting kicked over and footsteps pounding across hardwood. Emma also heard the noise and waved for Cal's attention. He looked down at her but kept his ear to the vent.

"Are you threatening me, you South American prick?!" the first voice shouted. "You don't know who you are fucking with! I don't care how you handle business south of the border, but up here in the states we don't make threats unless we are prepared to carry them out. I dare you to try something with me!"

Other voices rose to calm the angry man. The noise subsided. Cal heard wooden legs hit the floor as the chair was set upright.

Gallo spoke again.

"Take care of your business and there will be no problem." Then, under his breath, "pinche."

Cal barely made out the mumbled slur.

"Pinche to you, too, guy," the angry man retorted. "Just no more screw ups and let's put this whole ordeal behind us, okay?"

The room filled with sounds of agreement. It appeared the meeting was coming to a close.

Cal looked down at Emma. She was watching with rapt attention, dying to know what he was hearing.

"What are they saying?!" she whispered loudly.

Cal slowly stepped off the toilet tank. But, before he could reach the seat, his foot slipped, and the porcelain lid slid off the tank and crashed on the tile floor. The smash ricocheted loudly throughout the bathroom. Cal froze.

"Get down!" Emma said as the sound of men's voices filled the hallway. Cal hopped off the toilet and grabbed Emma in an embrace just as the bathroom door swung open.

"Occupied, old boy," Cal spoke to the man standing in the open doorway. He was a swarthy, meathead with forearms the size of hams. Clearly a bodyguard of some kind. He grunted in response to Cal's greeting and stared them down.

"My dear, I believe he really has to go," Cal said to Emma. They broke from their embrace and headed for the door. "Must be the shrimp cocktail."

The bodyguard watched their every move. As they slid past him, Cal patted his shoulder. He nodded at the smashed toilet and said, "The good news is you probably can't hurt it more than it already is."

Once they had successfully passed their new friend, Cal followed Emma back down the hallway and into the crowded room.

"Whew, that was close!" Emma said when they had rejoined the party and gotten out of earshot of the hulking bodyguard.

"Yeah, I got the impression that guy is not very friendly."

"So what were they saying? Could you hear them?" Emma asked excitedly.

"Loud and clear. They were—"

Cal paused as two couples squeezed past them en route to the back door. They smiled and nodded. When they had passed, he continued.

"They were up to no good. Something about a horse with 50 to 1 odds and they were all colluding over the plan. I couldn't make out exactly what was going on, but I am certain there is some kind of foul play underway."

"They are all working together?"

"That was my impression. There was some disagreement over a mistake that was made and then they resolved to finish the job and reap whatever reward it would bring. I'm telling you; this was not a light-hearted conversation among friends. They are plotting something. And our brush in the hallway with ol' Tiny proves they aren't taking any chances."

"50 to 1 odds? That is obviously referring to a horse race. But why would they be so concerned about manipulating a racehorse's odds? Unless…do you think they are planning to fix the…"

Emma trailed off as she realized the magnitude of her accusation. Could the outcome of a horse race watched by millions of people be swayed by a handful of corrupt owners?

Cal saw the incredulity in her eyes, and he shared it. Over 200 million dollars would change hands in the course of about ten minutes next Saturday. To think that the race could possibly be fixed…

He was just about to respond to Emma and confirm her suspicions when he saw the big bodyguard again from across the party. He was standing with a distinguished, olive-skinned man who wore a pencil mustache and donned a black velvet tuxedo jacket. Cal recognized him to be Augusto Gallo.

The bodyguard was looking in their direction and pointing his finger. As he did so, he leaned into Gallo's ear and spoke. Gallo looked up over the crowded room and followed the pointed index finger of his bodyguard. He and Cal made eye contact over the heads of the partygoers.

"Don't panic, but we have been made. The meathead just pointed us out to Gallo."

"Oh no. Are we in trouble?"

"I don't think so. He has no idea who we are. Remember we are Frank and Suzanne Diamond to everyone at the party. We just need to play it cool and keep up the game."

Emma nodded but Cal could see she was nervous. He was nervous too. He glanced around the room, trying to decide whether he should leave or stay. Where was Harper?

No, he thought to himself. I came here to talk to Gallo, so this is good. This is an opportunity. Stay confident and use it to your advantage.

No sooner had Cal made up his mind to stay than Gallo stepped off the stair he was using as a vantage point to survey the room and began making his way through the crowd. His bodyguard led the way, parting people in front of him so Gallo could walk unmolested.

"Hear he comes. Stay calm. We've got this."

The meathead approached with a look in his eyes like he wanted to rip them apart. He stopped about two feet away from Cal and Emma and froze, staring at them without saying a word.

Gallo appeared behind him.

"That is enough now, Manolo. These are guests at the party, and we want to make them feel welcome."

As Gallo spoke, he placed a hand on the bodyguard's shoulder and moved him to the side so he could address Cal and Emma. His accent was thick, and he spoke with the supreme confidence of a very wealthy man.

"Good evening, my friends. You must excuse my man, Manolo. He is, how do you say, *protective*."

For a few seconds, no one spoke. Then Cal answered.

"We just met in the bathroom, in fact. He is an intense chap." Then, he turned to Manolo. "Everything come out okay in there, old boy?"

Manolo grunted. He flexed his enormous chest. The muscles rippled beneath his tightly cut suit. He continued sizing Cal up.

"Pardon his English. It is not so good," Gallo responded. "Manolo tells me you were visiting the library earlier. Did you find what you were looking for?" This time he was addressing Emma directly.

"Um, yes. We were, just, uh…" Emma stammered.

Gallo cut in. "Forgive me. My manners. We have not even met and here I begin an interrogation. My name is Augusto Gallo. I come from Argentina to watch the Derby. Kentucky is a great state, no?"

"Indeed it is," Cal responded. "And you are being modest. We know who you are. The camera loves you. You will be on TV all day next week. And you have a horse running in the race, do you not?"

"Ah, you flatter. My reputation precedes." Gallo smiled slyly. "Yes, I do have a competitor, though my odds this year are maybe not so good. We shall see, as they say."

He closed his eyes and bowed his head slightly before continuing to speak.

"And you? Manolo and I do not recognize you at these parties. Please. Let us meet."

"Of course. You are correct in that this is our first visit to the Bonnycastle Gala. We are pleased to be in attendance. I am Frank Diamond, and this is my wife Suzanne."

Cal motioned to Emma and extended his hand to Gallo.

Gallo looked at Cal's outstretched hand but did not accept it.

"Diamond, eh? An interesting name no doubt. Tell me, Mr. Diamond, what do you do?"

"Well, lots of things, but mainly we are investors. We find small startup companies and help them grow so we all make money."

Gallo looked back at Cal. He seemed to be turning that concept over in his head, deciding whether the man in front of him was hiding something.

A sudden commotion occurred nearby. The crowd parted as a man came barreling toward the small group with his hand raised above his head. Everyone flinched except Manolo who flashed in front of his employer with the speed of an Olympic sprinter.

"Gallo, old buddy, have you met Frank?" came the disrupter's boisterous voice. Cal felt a hard slap on the shoulder. It was Stephen Zipper and he had clearly imbibed his share of the open bar.

Gallo looked at Stephen with disdain as though he had just been interrupted from a deep sleep. Stephen didn't seem to notice. He continued his jovial address.

"Yeah, old Frank and I are meeting next week to talk about outfitting my A/C units with internet technology. How are the units working out for you, by the way?"

Stephen slapped Gallo on the shoulder and turned back to Cal.

"We shipped 500 units to Buenos Aires in December. You know the month of December is the middle of summer for them. Got to keep those ponies cool, am I right?"

"Yes, Zeep. The horses have appreciated your invention. We thank you again."

Gallo was trying to get rid of Stephen, but Zip was not taking the hint.

"Say, Augusto, you should get in on this deal with Frankie and me. We're going to make a killing!"

Gallo nodded and responded cautiously, "We shall see."

As he spoke, Gallo signaled subtly to Manolo. The bodyguard immediately went into action. He grabbed Zip under the arm and ushered him away from the group. As he did, the two men bumped against Emma, knocking the glass from her hand and sending it shattering on the floor. Nearby guests turned to see the cause of the crashing noise.

Gallo began to get uncomfortable at the attention garnered by the commotion. He glanced about and smiled nervously at those who had turned to investigate the noise.

A few feet away, Zipper was stumbling to keep up with Manolo's forceful pace.

"Hey, now, just a minute. Is this any way to treat a business partner? I thought we were friends!" Zip was saying as Manolo dragged him toward the door.

Gallo looked away from Zipper and turned his attention back to Cal and Emma. He regained control of the situation and continued.

"A nice man, but he lacks self-control." Gallo dismissed the incident with a wave of his hand.

With his hand still in the air, Gallo snapped his fingers. Within seconds, a server appeared carrying a tray with three glasses of champagne.

Gallo removed one glass from the tray and waited for Cal and Emma to take the other two.

"Let us drink to good fortune and victory next week," he spoke as he tilted his glass to the air.

Cal and Emma raised their new glasses and joined in Gallo's toast.

"Here, here. May the best man win," said Cal. He looked Gallo in the eye and drank.

Gallo smiled and drained his own glass of champagne just as Manolo was returning to the group.

"You must excuse me, Mr. and Mrs. Diamond. I have to be going. A pleasure to meet you both."

And with those final words, he turned and left the room with Manolo close at his heels.

"I trust him about as far as I can throw him," Cal said as soon as Gallo had walked away.

"Yeah, he's shady. Did you get the impression he knew more about us than he pretended to?"

"I did. The whole conversation felt like a test. I hope we passed."

"Will you investigate him more?"

"I don't want to, but I think I have to. Something tells me this race-fixing caper is connected to Halcott's death."

"You didn't really get to ask many questions this time. He did all the talking."

"Exactly. And then that goofball Zipper showed up and derailed everything. It seemed like he spooked Gallo and prompted him to disappear," Cal said. He was disappointed. "I was really hoping to mention Sterling Halcott's name and get a read on Gallo's body language."

"Should we try to find him again?"

"I don't think so. It might look suspicious if we force it. Unless you have an idea?" he asked.

He looked at Emma and, as he did, a droplet of sweat trickled down his temple. He reached up to wipe his brow.

"It's hot in here with all of these people, isn't it?"

Cal wasn't feeling well. His face was hot. He tugged at the collar of his tuxedo. He could see the concern in Emma's eyes.

"Cal, you don't look so good. Let's get some air."

"It's Frank..." Cal replied, but his voice was weak. The room was spinning. The voices around him became garbled. It sounded like he was in a tunnel.

Emma grabbed his arm and tried to lead him toward the door.

"Were you sneaking drinks behind my back?" she goaded. "Or maybe you had the shrimp cocktail?"

Cal tried to smile, but the room was darkening. His peripheral vision was disappearing completely. All he could see was Emma in front of him and beyond her was the back door. It was a million miles away. He lunged for her shoulder and missed.

"This man is about to be sick!" a woman screamed. The people around Cal parted with a gasp.

Cal stood still, wavering on his weakening knees. He tried to call Emma's name, but his mouth couldn't form the words. He looked at her with pleading eyes. He was going down.

At the last minute, over Emma's shoulder, Cal spotted Manolo standing in the corner by the door. Cal's vision was a blur, but he could tell Manolo was watching him and smiling.

Suddenly Cal realized what was happening. He extended his arm and slapped the champagne glass from Emma's hand just as the room began spiraling out of control. Then everything went black and he crumpled to the floor.

23

Cal opened his eyes.

Stone walls. Dim lights. Dripping water.

The air was musty and damp. Humid but chilly. A sickening, earthy smell like moss or mushrooms mixed with urine.

He tried to sit up. His head pounded, and he felt dizzy, so he slumped back down on the cold, hard slab that supported him.

His eyes adjusted to the dark room. He attempted to gain his bearings.

Where was he? What happened? How did he get here?

The pain coursing through his skull was blinding. He reached for his head and cradled it with his hands, hoping to make the throbbing subside. He curled his knees to his chest and shivered in the cool, moist air.

He slipped back into unconsciousness.

He awoke again sometime later to the sound of voices. The dim light previously streaming from a hole near the ceiling was gone. In its place, the area was lit by a single, naked bulb hanging from a black cord in the corner of the room.

Cal laid still and listened to the voices. They were speaking Spanish. He couldn't make out everything they were saying, but he picked up bits and pieces.

"Why can't we just kill him and get it over with? I'm tired of sitting here."

"Because El Señor says so. Stop asking questions. ¿Tienes los sietes?"

"Pescaté."

Cal raised up on one elbow and squinted his eyes to see across the dark room.

Two men sat at a wooden table. The lightbulb hung just above their heads. It illuminated the tabletop and Cal could see they were both holding cards. There was a discard pile between them with a stack of cards face down. Each man had a glass full of amber liquid, and a dusty liquor bottle rested uncorked and half-empty on the table next to the pile of cards.

The dirty floor at their feet was littered with cigarette butts. Both men had a burning cigarette protruding from their bearded mouths. Smoke hung heavy over the table. It thickened the air below the lightbulb and shrouded the card players and their rum bottle in a hazy cloud.

The men heard him awaken. They shifted in their chairs to watch him. Laughing and prodding, they teased him about his disheveled appearance.

"Despiértaté, gringo. Buenos dias. You sleep good?"

Cal tried to speak, but his throat felt like it was full of sand. He cleared it with a rasping cough.

"Water?" he croaked.

The men laughed again. Then one of them stood up from the table and reached for a bucket on the floor next to them. He dipped a ladle into the bucket. When he withdrew the ladle, it was filled to the brim with liquid.

The man walked toward Cal carrying the ladle. Water sloshed over the lip with each step and splashed on the concrete floor.

Cal licked his cracked lips in anticipation. His mouth was parched.

As the guard approached, Cal could see he carried a revolver tucked into his waistband. The handle of the pistol was exposed. The man rested his left hand on the gun as he walked toward Cal.

The guard stopped a few feet from Cal. He extended the ladle, keeping his left hand on the gun.

Cal reached out for the ladle, but the man withdrew it. He shook his head.

When the ladle was extended again, Cal leaned forward to drink. The man tilted it to Cal's lips. He managed a few swallows before the guard tipped the ladle and dumped the rest of the water into his lap.

The water tasted bitter, but Cal was too thirsty to care. He slumped back against the wall and watched the man return to his position at the table.

"Where am I?" Cal asked after a few seconds. "¿Dónde estoy?"

The men looked up from their card game.

"You a long way from home, gringo. A long way from home."

"Who are you? Why am I here?"

"You mess with the wrong people, pinche. You make big mistake."

Cal sat quietly for a few minutes and tried to piece together the events that brought him here. His head was still cloudy, and he was having trouble seeing straight.

Then it hit him. He remembered the Bonnycastle party and meeting Gallo. He remembered getting dizzy and then…what happened after that? He couldn't remember anything after that moment.

He allowed his head to loll back against the stone wall behind him. He closed his eyes and his mind drifted. The voices of the men slowly faded into the distance. He sat up straight when a sudden memory shot into his brain.

Emma! The champagne! Gallo had drugged them with the champagne toast. That was it. Oh no, Emma!

"Is the lady here? ¿Dónde está ella?" Cal croaked through his dry, split lips.

The men stopped playing again. They looked at each other solemnly. Neither spoke.

"¡Dimeló!" Cal shouted with all the energy he could muster.

"Don't worry, gringo. She in a safe place."

Oh no, Cal thought. What have I done? The worst-case scenario has come true and now I have endangered the woman I care about. What am I going to do now?

Then another thought entered his mind. If he wanted to get out of here, he first had to learn just where *here* was. He remembered Gallo's home country.

"Is this Buenos Aires?" he asked.

"Sí."

"How long have I been here?"

"Trés dias."

"So that makes this...Tuesday?"

"Sí."

Three days? He must have been drugged heavily. Or else they had kept him under by giving him more of the toxic mixture. Gallo. Damn it. He knew he couldn't trust him. He had to find Emma and get her out of there.

"Let me talk to your boss. Where is Gallo?"

No response from the men. They continued playing cards.

"¡¿Dónde está Gallo?!" Cal shouted.

The second man laid down his cards. He stood up from the table and walked out of the room.

The first man kept his eyes on Cal. He sat with his chair leaned against the stone wall. One foot rested on the cold, concrete floor. His left hand grazed the handle of the revolver in his waistband.

The two men stared at each other silently, waiting.

After a few minutes, Cal heard the sound of footsteps in the hallway. He sat up and did his best to clear his head and look like he had it together.

The second guard entered the room. He stepped aside and stood to the right of the door. Gallo entered next. He hesitated in the doorway for a moment, waiting for his eyes to adjust to the dim lighting.

He spotted Cal seated on the concrete slab and smiled.

"How are you enjoying your stay so far?" he sneered.

"Where is the mujer?"

"My, my. We are all business today, aren't we?"

"Gallo, you asshole. What exactly do you think you are doing here? You have kidnapped two Americans. There is no chance you will get away with this."

"Oh, but I already have, Mr. Diamond. Or should I say, *Mr. Tyson.*"

Gallo paused to allow his discovery to sink in before proceeding.

"Yes, you might be accustomed to dealing with amateurs in your little sleuthing business, but I am not one. You have picked the wrong man to fuck with and now you are paying the price."

The guards looked at each other and snickered. One spoke in broken English to Cal.

"I tell you. You make big mistake."

He looked at the other guard and they both laughed again.

"Shut the fuck up, you imbeciles." Gallo silenced them with a word. "Bring the girl in here."

The guards straightened up and exchanged a glance. "¡Ahora! ¡Damelá!"

The two men shuffled out of the room, leaving Cal and Gallo alone.

Cal stared up at Gallo. He wanted to stand but he was afraid his knees were too weak to support him.

"It was the champagne, wasn't it? You drugged us."

"Come now. Let us not point fingers. You should be thanking Manolo you didn't crack your skull on the floor. He caught you when you fell."

"Right. I'd like to thank him personally with a left hook."

Gallo thought this was funny. He laughed loudly and leaned his hand on one of the chairs. His smile disappeared in an instant and his expression became as hard as the stone on which he stood.

"I assure you, Mr. Tyson, Manolo would rip you to shreds in a matter of seconds. Perhaps we should bring him in here and let you have a go…"

"Maybe later." Cal didn't want to get ahead of himself. He knew he had no hope of overcoming Gallo and his goons in his current state. "Tell me what you plan to do with us."

"In due time, gringo. In due time. Let us not forget you brought this on yourself. If you could have kept your nose out of my business, you would not be here."

Cal looked away. He was dealing with a psychopath. No sense trying to reason with him. He thought for a minute and then looked up at Gallo.

"Did you kill Sterling Halcott?"

Gallo was unfazed by the pointed question. He reached into his jacket pocket and calmly withdrew a gold cigarette case. He removed a cigarette, placed it in his mouth, and struck a match.

Raising the lighted match to his cigarette, he inhaled and drew a breath of smoke into his lungs. He exhaled the smoke across the room in Cal's direction.

Before extinguishing the match, he leaned over to the guards' table and lit a candle next to the bottle of rum.

Gallo stared into the candle flame as it flickered on the table in front of him. The room seemed to grow darker. Gallo smoked his cigarette. No one spoke. Cal could hear the sounds of nature creeping in through the missing rock in the wall above him. Dense, thick, wild, nature. He hoped for a horn honk or car wheels, anything to indicate the presence of humanity. Instead he heard nothing but crickets and birds hearkening the approach of night.

Finally, Gallo turned back to Cal and replied.

"What if I say yes? You are not exactly in a position to do anything about it now, are you?"

He was right and Cal knew it. Still Cal ignored Gallo's obfuscation and pressed him.

"Why did you do it? You and Halcott were probably the two wealthiest men in the horse racing business."

Gallo drew again from the cigarette. He was in no hurry to explain himself to his captive. He was toying with Cal like a cat might play with a mouse before finally slaughtering it. The mouse scurries a few feet before the cat slams its clawed paws into the mouse's flesh and draws it back in.

"Eventually a man reaches the point where money has no meaning..." Gallo trailed off. He seemed to be thinking about his last statement, letting it wash over the room. His eyes stared into the candle flame as though it held the answers to life's deepest questions. "Do you know what is always more important than money?" he finally asked.

Cal was not interested in entertaining the philosophical musings of a madman, but he wanted to hear Gallo's confession. He wanted Gallo to admit with his own words he had orchestrated the murder of Sterling Halcott. He waited for Gallo to continue.

"Power, my friend. Power is the highest form of currency for the wealthy. Collecting more money...to me...it no longer thrills. But more power? Yes, a man can always gain more power."

Great, Cal thought. Not only a psycho but a megalomaniac. He pushed Gallo to continue.

"OK. But what does that have to do with Halcott?"

Gallo needed no time to ponder his response to this question.

"The only thing that can stop a powerful man is another man of equal or greater power."

"I see. So Halcott got in your way?"

"Sterling allowed morality to influence his decisions. He was a product of your American South. Too many morals. Too much chivalry."

Cal bristled at this comment but remained quiet. Might as well let Gallo keep talking.

"There is a time for principles and a time for action. One should not let one's principles interfere with the need for action."

"I'm not sure the two are mutually exclusive," Cal retorted.

Gallo poured a glass of the amber liquor the guards had been drinking. He raised it in a mock toast to Cal and took a sip. He rolled the liquid on his tongue before expelling it with a forceful spit. The alcohol splattered on the concrete between them, splashing across Cal's leg. He could smell the strong grain of the booze. Like rubbing alcohol, it burned his nostrils and sent a shudder through his chest.

"Fucking piss water," Gallo spat again to clear the rum from his mouth. He threw the empty glass against the stone wall. It shattered with a loud crash and sent shards of glass ricocheting about the cell. The sound of broken glass echoed throughout the cavernous structure. For the first time, Cal gained a sense of the magnitude of the building in which he was being held captive. The reverberation exited the open door and rang down the hallway the guards had taken to fetch Emma. From the echo, Cal could tell the hallway was solid and long with no windows or escape hatch.

Shortly Gallo regained his composure and continued lecturing Cal.

"Gambling is a multibillion-dollar industry. And what are gambling's two most important minutes of the year?" Gallo asked the room rhetorically.

He got no response but continued speaking.

"Yes, there is the World Cup and fútbol Americano's Super Bowl. But nothing compares to the excitement packed into the two minutes of the Kentucky Derby. Millions of dollars change hands in 120 seconds. Do you understand how much power is held by a man who can influence the outcome of that race?"

Gallo looked at Cal. He wanted an acknowledgement. The candlelight flickered. Gallo's moustache glistened with drops of rum and saliva.

"The lives of millions of people will be affected in a split second," Cal finally replied.

"Exactamente. You are learning, hijo."

"So you *are* planning to fix the Derby?"

Gallo's face contorted at the accusation. He seemed pained by the implication Cal had just lobbed at him.

"Fix is not a pretty word. We are going to, how do you say, *help* the Derby. Imagine the world's excitement when my horse, Calavera, with 50 to 1 odds, crosses the finish line first?"

Cal shook his head slowly in disbelief. Gallo had finally admitted his true motive.

"*Cincuenta a uno,*" Gallo repeated for emphasis. "So thrilling. People will talk about it for years."

"And you and your cronies will rake in a huge pot I'm sure."

"It is true, but remember, for me, it is not about money. I will be the man who changed history."

Spoken like a true psychopath, Cal thought. He had Gallo's own admission of the Derby tampering, but he also needed to tie that back to his case.

"OK. So what happened with Halcott then? He got in your way?"

"Many times we have worked together, but he could not be convinced to join us this time. He said the Derby was too sacred. He refused to participate. *Pinche maricón.* He fucked up our whole plan. He had to be dealt with."

Gallo stopped talking and turned his attention back to the candle flame.

For a while, neither man spoke. Each was waiting for the other to break the silence.

Cal began to get nervous. Gallo had just admitted to killing one of the highest profile men in the United States. He is insane. What is he going to do with us?

Just then, Cal heard a door slam in the outer hallway. He sat up and listened, quickly recognizing the voice of Emma. His heart sank to learn she was not back in Kentucky safe and sound, but he was glad to know she was alive.

"Get your hands off me, you disgusting prick!" Her voice echoed through the hall.

She soon appeared in the doorway of Cal's cell with a guard gripping each arm.

"She is feisty, boss. You want us to shut her up?" the first guard asked.

"Put her over there," Gallo responded. He indicated toward the concrete slab where Cal was seated.

The men grabbed her arms and dragged her toward the back of the cell. She quickly spotted Cal and gasped with relief.

"Cal! What are we going to do?" she exhaled.

"Don't worry. He will never get away with it," Cal assured her.

Gallo laughed quietly. The guards cautiously joined in his laughter.

"Mr. Tyson, have you not yet learned I get away with anything I want? I will allow nothing to interfere with my plan. We are only five days away from setting history."

Emma looked at Cal. "What is he talking about?" she asked nervously.

"I'll tell you later."

"You better talk fast, Mr. Tyson. You will soon run out of words."

Cal and Emma exchanged a quick glance and swallowed hard.

Gallo turned to the guards and issued orders.

"Hold them here until I decide how to get rid of them. Don't let them talk. I will be back mañana."

And with that, he turned and exited the cell. The steel door slammed behind him.

The guards took their seats at the table. One poured a shot of rum into the remaining glass and the other took a slug directly from the bottle. They picked up the cards that were lying face down where they had left them.

Cal and Emma sat silently on the concrete slab. They stared at the dark and dirty floor of the cell, wondering if they would ever see Kentucky again.

24

"What did he say? What are we going to do?" Emma whispered with fear in her eyes.

"He did it. He killed Halcott and he is planning to fix the Derby. We have to get out of here."

"¡Cállete!" the first guard shouted. "No talking."

Cal and Emma froze. They sat quietly and waited for the guards to resume their card game. The candle flickered on the table. The second guard cleared his throat and spat on the stone floor.

After a few minutes, the guards were laughing again and drinking from the bottle of rum. Cal risked another whisper.

"Were you able to see anything from the hallway? Any doors or windows?"

"There is a door at the end of the hallway, but how are we even going to get out of this room?"

Cal scanned the walls for a sign. There had to be a way out.

The cell's heavy steel door had a keyhole that would flip the lock from the inside, but the key was nowhere in sight. There was a window high above them near the ceiling. But even if they could reach it, bars covered the glass and it was too small to slip through.

There were no possible exits other than the window and the door. And both of those were blocked.

"The guards must have a key to that door," Cal mouthed to Emma.

She didn't hear him. She was deep in thought.

"Hey, are you with me?"

Still no response. She sat quietly on the bench and stared at the stone floor.

Her silence worried Cal. They would both need to be in peak mental shape if they were going to get out alive. If she gave up, they were both lost.

Cal leaned over to pat Emma's knee. Before he could reach her, she stood up and brushed past his outstretched hand.

"Emma, what are you doing?" Cal asked nervously.

Emma gave no answer. She stood next to him, hesitating for a split second. Then she strolled toward the guards. She called out to them as she moved.

"Hey, boys. Who's winning?"

The guards immediately turned around. The first guard pulled the pistol from his waistband and leveled it at Emma.

"¡Siénteté!"

"¿Por qué, señor? I'm bored. Just making conversation."

Cal lowered his head into his hands, half cursing and half praying. He hoped Emma had a plan because otherwise they were both dead.

"¡Siénteté ahora! Sit down immediately or I will put a bullet in your head!"

Emma ignored the threat and continued advancing toward the guards' table. Cal couldn't believe his eyes.

"How's about you give me a shot of that rum. I need to take the edge off a little."

She was only a few feet away from the first guard now. His pistol was pointed directly at her chest. He stared at her, stone faced and silent, with his index finger on the trigger.

Emma smiled at him. She showed no sign of backing down.

The first guard was in disbelief. He didn't know what to do. He glanced at the second guard as if to ask for advice. The second guard shrugged. Everyone stared at each other. No one spoke. It was a standoff.

Cal held his breath. The guard's eyes were glazed and red. He was squinting in the musty darkness, staring at the woman who so nonchalantly approached him and his cocked pistol.

The seated guard was also staring at Emma. He lowered his eyes to her waist, down to her legs and her bare toes that gripped the stone floor beneath her. They were painted with blue nail polish and caked in dust from the dirty prison floor. Cal realized for the first time the heels she had worn to the party were long gone. She had been barefoot for three days in this dank dungeon.

The armed guard licked his lips. His face loosened up as he slowly lowered the gun. He laughed louder and louder until his whole body was shaking hysterically. This 120-pound blonde presented no threat. She was no match for her two burly captors. In fact, maybe they could have a little fun with her before they kill her. He grabbed the bottle of rum from the table and held it out.

"Drink, chica. You get drunk. Drink, drink."

As he spoke, he took a step forward and shook the bottle in his hand.

Emma took another step toward the guard and reached for the bottle with her left hand. The guard pulled it back before she could grab it.

"Ah ah," he waved his finger at her. He spoke in a scolding manner, "No, no. This not for ladies. Too strong for you I think." He looked over to his partner and joked, "Ya esta borracha?" They both laughed loudly.

Emma dropped her hand to her hip and waited for the joke to run its course.

"You sure, ella?" he asked. "Maybe the drink make you do crazy things you don't want to…"

He shook the bottle again.

This time as the guard shook his bottle, Cal heard the jingle of keys. He followed the sound and spotted the metal key ring dangling from the drunken guard's belt. Bingo. There is our ticket out of here.

Meanwhile, the guards were riffing in Spanish and laughing. The man with the bottle finally handed Emma the liquor. She took the neck of the bottle in one hand and held it up to the naked lightbulb.

Even from ten feet away, Cal could see the silt swirling in the bottom of the bottle. No way in hell he would drink that swill.

Emma sniffed the liquor. She shrugged her shoulders and raised the bottle to her lips. The men watched with lustful eyes as she tilted the bottle of rum back and swallowed the golden liquid.

The guards cheered her on while she drank.

She immediately handed the bottle to the second guard and admonished him to follow her lead. The second guard raised the bottle to his lips, but the first guard—the one with the keys—snatched it from his hands and drank instead. The two men were fighting over who would be the first to drink after this daring muchacha.

Once both men had taken a turn, Emma grabbed the bottle again and immediately started another round.

Cal watched incredulously. Whatever Emma was doing seemed to be working. On the bright side, if they could get the guards drunk, they might be able to take advantage of their temporary weakness.

As Emma continued passing the bottle with the guards, Cal reached down and started to carefully ease the laces out of his right shoe. He was still wearing his tuxedo from the party, though it was tattered and covered in dirt.

"Keep them entertained, Emma," he thought.

Right on cue, Emma began dancing around the cell with the bottle in her hand. Her cocktail dress swung side to side, spiraling around her bare legs. The guards watched her every move in a trance.

Cal pulled the shoelace through its final eyelet and wrapped it around his hands, which he then rested in his lap.

Emma spun to face Cal. Her back was to the guards now. They were entranced by her swaying hips. Back and forth like a pendulum in front of them.

She looked at Cal with wide eyes. He nodded and lifted the rope shoelace from his lap to show her he was ready.

Without a moment's hesitation, Emma whipped around with the bottle raised high in her hand and smashed it into the head of the first guard before he could react. The bottle hit his skull with a dull thwack, and he slumped to the floor unconscious.

As soon as Emma made contact, Cal jumped into action. He caught the second guard as he was standing up from his chair. Cal wrapped the shoelace around the guard's neck and yanked backwards.

The guard struggled against the tightening cord, but Cal's grip was too much for his drunken flailing. Gradually, his writhing subsided until his weight dropped into Cal's arms and he stopped moving.

In a matter of seconds, both guards lay on the floor, out cold. One at Emma's feet and one at Cal's.

"Where did you learn that trick?" Cal asked incredulously.

"When I tended bar, every loser in the place wanted to buy me a shot. Trust me, I can drink these clowns under the table any day."

She winked at Cal, and just to rub it in, she took another slug from the rum bottle before slamming it down on the wooden table.

"One for the road," Cal said as he turned the first guard over and yanked the key ring from his belt. "Now let's hope one of these keys unlocks the door."

He grabbed the guard's pistol and tucked it into his own waistband. The third key was the charm and the lock clicked into place. The door swung open with a creak and Cal slowly peeked into the hallway.

"All clear," he whispered.

He entered the hall with Emma right on his heels.

The hallway was even darker than the cell they had just left. No windows. The only light in the corridor came from a bulb hanging on each end of the stone-walled passage. They headed left toward one of the bulbs.

They passed more doors that led to holding rooms similar to the one in which they were captive for the last three days. Cal wondered if there were other prisoners behind those doors. The stench of urine permeated the dank dungeon. Their footsteps echoed in the corridor as they ran.

At the end of the hall was another door. When they reached it, Cal placed his ear against the door and listened for sound coming from the other side.

He could hear faint voices. He made eye contact with Emma and raised a finger to his lips. He continued listening.

"A la semana próxima en *Alma Pirata…*"

He could hear people arguing, followed by dramatic music.

Cal chuckled. A telenovela. The voices were coming from a television.

He turned the handle and eased the door open just wide enough to see through the open crack.

The television sat across the room on a counter. The volume was turned up loud. Commercials in Spanish entered the corridor through the open crack in the door.

Cal slowly scanned the room. He swept his eyes around the perimeter, searching for signs of life. The room was empty other than the blaring television. He pushed the door open and snuck inside. Emma was right on his heels.

Once inside, the two searched for their next step.

This room had windows along one wall. The world outside was dark. A bright moon overhead lit the grounds enough to reveal they were surrounded by jungle. Fifty feet from the building, the manicured lawn quickly receded into a mass of trees and dense undergrowth.

Cal stepped up to the window. He cupped his hands around his eyes to peer outside.

"Are there more guards out there?" Emma whispered.

"I can't see any from here, but I am willing to bet there are. If we can get to the tree line without being spotted, me might be safe."

"But then what? I mean, where the heck are we?"

"According to the guards, we are somewhere near Buenos Aires," Cal answered.

"OK, that means we must be close to water."

"Right. I'm guessing the ocean is one way and the city is the other. Not quite sure which is which. Or, for that matter, which is worse," said Cal.

Emma nodded. She knew they had to risk it. "Let's pick one and hope for the best. It's either that or we can hang out here and chat with Gallo in the morning."

"Do you think he serves Argentinian coffee to his guests?"

The look on Emma's face showed she was not amused.

Cal pressed on the window. It gave way, opening outward on its hinges.

The sounds of the jungle rushed in through the open window. The property was alive with the hum of insects and birds. Cool, salty air filled their lungs, telling them the ocean was close by.

Cal offered Emma a leg up and she climbed out of the open window into the darkness.

She was straddling the windowsill with one leg in and one leg out when they heard a noise coming from an adjacent room. They both froze in fear. Jangling of keys and shoes scuffling across the dusty floor. A toilet flushed in the next room. They were about to have company.

"Go!" he said as Emma swung her other leg out the window. He lowered her the final few feet to the grass below.

"What about you?"

"I'll be fine. Get to the tree line and wait. If I don't follow in five minutes, leave without me."

She looked up at him for a second, her eyes pleading. Then she turned and ran into the darkness.

Cal closed the window and took a position behind the bathroom door. He could hear the newcomer's belt jingling on the other side. They would be face to face in seconds. Cal pressed himself against the wall. He pulled the revolver from his waistband and waited.

The tiny gap under the bathroom door went from yellow to black as the light switched off. The door opened.

The guard stepped out of the bathroom and stretched with a yawn. He scratched his belly and walked toward a chair in front of the television. He passed Cal's hiding place behind the door. Cal silently fell in pace with the guard. He crept up behind him and grabbed the guard around the neck. He pressed the revolver to the guard's head and hissed into his ear.

"¡Cálleté! ¡No se mueva!"

The guard froze.

"¿Dónde está el mar?" Cal asked.

Cal could smell the stale sweat on the guard's collar as he gripped his throat from behind. He held him tightly so the guard could not shout for help. The pistol remained cocked in his right hand, pressed firmed against the man's head.

"¡Digamé ahora!"

The guard slowly raised a finger, solemnly pointing out the direction to the ocean as Cal had requested.

Cal surveyed the guard's desk until he spotted a set of handcuffs. He grabbed them and dragged the guard back into the bathroom he had just vacated.

He knocked the guard to the bathroom floor and aimed the gun at him. The guard lay there looking up at Cal. He bent over and cuffed the man to a pipe that ran under the sink. He waved the gun for emphasis and placed a finger to his lips. Then he slowly backed out of the room. As he did, he kept the gun trained on the guard.

Cal stepped slowly backward the whole way to the wall. When he reached the window, he pushed it open. He tossed the revolver into the grass and hopped up on the windowsill. With one final glance back at the handcuffed guard, Cal lowered himself to the ground.

The jungle was even louder once Cal was outside. He waited for a second to get his bearings and let his eyes adjust to the moonlight.

The jungle noise was like no other sound Cal had heard in the states. The thrum of insects drowned out everything. The air was thick, but the night breeze was cool against his skin. He turned and ran for the edge of the jungle, searching its perimeter for a sign from Emma.

Just as he reached the tree line, the yard behind him flooded with light. Their escape had been discovered!

"Cal! Over here!"

It was Emma. She was waving for him. He could barely hear her over the sound of the jungle. He caught up to her and shouted, "Run!"

They took off in the direction the guard had identified as leading to the ocean. Gallo's men were hot on their trail, but they didn't wait around to find out.

As soon as they penetrated the canopy of the jungle, the darkness pressed in around them. The light from the house faded away until only the faint glow of the moon lit their path.

A thin walkway had been cut through the undergrowth and they rushed down it. Cal hoped this trail would lead them to the water. The two ran along the path with everything they had. They knew being caught would carry dire consequences.

After a few hundred yards, the path opened up and the jungle floor turned to sand. They had hit the beach. The trees became more and more sparse until they reached the mouth of the jungle and exploded out from under the canopy.

As soon as they escaped the tree cover, the moon illuminated the entire beach. They could see the ocean in front of them. The moon's pale light glinted on the crest of each soft wave.

Before them a long, wooden dock extended into the water. At its end a small seaplane bobbed peacefully in the tide.

"Come on!" Cal shouted. He pointed to the plane.

"Can you fly?" Emma was gasping for air.

Cal didn't respond. He just kept running.

They reached the end of the dock and Cal yanked open the door of the seaplane. He ushered Emma inside and climbed in after her.

He took a seat at the controls. Flipping switches, pulling levers. He tried to get his bearings.

"I knew a guy who had one of these in college and we flew it together a few times. How hard can it be?"

"Are you kidding me? Oh my—"

The rest of Emma's words were drowned out by the sound of the seaplane's engine roaring into action. The propeller began spinning. Cal slipped off the rope that anchored the plane to the dock.

He glanced back at the tree line of the beach once more. Flashlights bounced and swirled in the darkness near the canopy exit. Gallo's men had found them!

"Hurry!" shouted Emma over the roar of the engine. She was on her knees in the passenger seat, facing backward in the small plane. She watched out the window at the men who were running up the dock after them.

The plane began coasting along the water as they headed out to sea. They were in a small cove. Gallo's private beach. The gulf was surrounded by greenery and eventually it opened into the Atlantic Ocean directly in front of them.

The flashlights were now bouncing up the dock, headed right for them.

The plane chugged along. They picked up speed as they approached the open waters.

"They're coming!"

Just as the men reached the end of the dock, the plane's nose edged out of the water. Cal pulled the throttle fully open. The rudders tilted and the floating skis lifted from the waves. Cal leaned back on the stick and suddenly they were airborne, heading in the direction of the cove's exit.

Gunfire sounded from the dock. Cal banked the plane to avoid it. Within seconds, they were safely out of range.

"We made it!" shouted Emma.

Once they were beyond the reach of Gallo's men, Cal banked again and veered left. He followed the green and blue warning lights on the docks below and turned the plane parallel to the coastline.

They could follow the beach of Uruguay back north, but the shortest distance to the states was due north over the South American continent. Cal hoped they could make it to Miami or at least Cuba before running out of fuel. He checked the cockpit dashboard to make sure the controls were all in working order. The fuel gauge was full. Everything checked out. He turned to Emma and gave a thumbs up.

Emma was in shock. She sat in the passenger seat with a look of terror in her eyes.

"What in the hell just happened?" she stammered.

Cal laughed grimly. He did his best to pretend all was well, but inside he felt exactly the same way. That was a close one.

PART II

25

On Thursday morning, Cal awakened in his own bed at his house in Lexington. Sunlight streamed in through the windows above his headboard and, for a few precious seconds, he forgot about the events that had transpired over the past week.

He stretched his legs in bed and yawned. He rolled over and glanced at the clock on the wall, which informed him it was 11:00 a.m. He let his eyes slide closed again.

But they quickly shot back open. He did a double take at the clock. 11:00! Did he sleep that late?! He sat up in bed with a start.

Then the memories came flooding back to him. He and Emma had arrived in Lexington in the middle of the night after a two-day trip back from Argentina.

When he laid down last night, he felt like he could sleep for a week. In fact, Cal was surprised it wasn't later once he remembered the circumstances of the previous evening.

The seaplane they had stolen from Gallo had gotten them as far as Miami, and not a mile further before running out of fuel. It was as though the plane's fuel tanks had been outfitted specifically for a flight of that distance.

Once in Miami, they bought tickets on a commercial flight for the remaining leg of the journey back to Lexington.

Lucky for them, Gallo's pilot had left an envelope full of cash in the plane. Cal preferred not to think about the origin of the money. But with their belongings confiscated, they had no choice other than to use the resources available to them.

They had landed just off the coast of South Beach and coasted to a public pier where they ditched the plane and waded up to the beach jammed full of sunbathers.

Cal smiled remembering the looks they got as they exited the ocean in their tattered and filthy evening attire.

A store on the strip provided new clothes courtesy of Gallo's cash. They devoured a meal before catching a cab to the airport for the second flight of their voyage—only this time they were passengers.

The plane had touched down at the Lexington airport around midnight and they were both ready to kiss the tarmac when they exited. It was a long trip, but they had finally made it.

As they bid a harried goodbye, Cal and Emma agreed they needed to lay low. Gallo would certainly have his men on the lookout for them.

When Cal hugged Emma goodbye, he was afraid it might be a while before they met again. After all, he had just put her through an experience not easily forgotten. She was tough, but they were both exhausted and needed a break from the action.

Emma took the rest of the week off at the library and headed to her parents' house in Louisville on Thursday morning to rest and avoid the public eye. Getting away from Gallo's reach was smart.

Cal lay exposed in his bed and wondered if he, too, should get out of dodge for a few days. If Gallo wanted to find him, he could. And with the dirt Cal now had on him, there was a good chance Gallo would be working hard to protect his interests.

Two days until the Derby. Cal had to stop Gallo from carrying out his plan. And he needed to figure out some way to alert the authorities about Gallo's part in Sterling Halcott's death.

Cal swung his feet over the side of the bed and sat up. Two days left. He had to make sure Gallo is caught in the act. Just a little bit more and then he could rest.

He stood up and walked into the bathroom where he hit the shower and began to formulate a plan.

When Cal stepped out of the shower, he heard his phone ringing in the den. It had been so long since his house phone rang that it took him a second to register the sound. Gallo had taken his cell phone. Anyone who wanted to reach him would have to use the landline. He wrapped a towel around his waist and went to see who was calling.

"Tyson here," he spoke into the receiver when he picked it up.

"Cal! What on earth happened to you?! Where have you been?!"

The voice on the other end of the line was Harper.

"It's a long story, but I've got our guy now. It's Gallo. Gallo killed your husband."

Harper gasped. She was silent for a moment.

"Are you sure?" she finally asked. "How do you know?"

"He told me point blank."

"What are you talking about? When?"

Cal had no idea where to begin.

"And whatever happened to you at the party?" Harper continued the interrogation. "One minute you were there and the next you were gone. My chauffeur said he drove the car home alone!"

"I'm telling you, it's a long story and I don't have time for the details right now. Gallo is still at large, and I am willing to bet he is getting desperate. Have you heard from him by any chance?"

"Not recently, Cal. I'm getting worried. Should I be worried? You are saying we were right? Sterling did not commit suicide?"

"Yes, I believe that to be true."

"Oh!" she gasped. "This is too much. What do we do? Can we stop him?"

"I apologize for laying all of this on you right now, but there's more. Gallo is plotting to fix the Derby. He plans to make his horse win after going off at 50 to 1 odds by somehow tampering with the rest of the field." Cal paused for a breath. "Does the name Calavera mean anything to you?"

"That is the name of Gallo's Derby runner," Harper answered.

"I was afraid of that."

"But how? How can he influence the other horses in the race?"

"I haven't gotten that far yet. Jubal Early mentioned something about doping horses. Maybe that is part of it."

Then Cal had another thought.

"What about jockeys?" he asked. "Is there any chance enough jockeys could be paid off to change the outcome of the race?"

"I just don't know. Most jockeys are honorable people from what I have seen. I would be surprised if Gallo could get to them."

"Hmmm…"

Cal was thinking. He needed to enter the mind of Gallo. How would he carry out this complex scheme?

"What about your jockey? Who will be riding Valkyrie? Is your horse still the favorite?"

"Yes, he is. And I certainly have no plans of pulling him from the race. Our jockey is Kyna Ryan. No one knows Valkyrie like she does."

"Do you trust her?"

Harper thought for a moment.

"I do trust her. She has been with Sterling and I for over five years. We have been grooming her for a Derby bid and this is her year. I don't know what Gallo has planned, but it will take a miracle for him to beat Kyna aboard Valkyrie."

Cal hesitated to respond. He was processing this information. He still wasn't sure exactly what to do next. He knew Gallo had to be caught red-handed on American

193

soil if any charges were going to stick. Otherwise, Cal's accusations would fall on deaf ears. Gallo would simply return to Argentina, and Cal would forever have to watch his back in fear of repercussions.

He knew what he had to do.

"Harper, will you take me to the Kentucky Derby? I need to get on Millionaires Row so I can have another crack at Gallo. And, for that matter, I believe you may be in danger until I can put him away for good. I would like to keep you close by for your safety."

"Oh my," she breathed. "I just don't know, Cal. Getting you into the Bonnycastle Gala was one thing, but taking you to Millionaires Row is another matter entirely. Everyone will be watching me. What will they think—only a month after my husband's death? I can't do it, Cal. I just can't. There must be another way."

Cal understood what she meant. He knew he was asking a lot. But he had to get in there, and, without an explicit invitation, he had no chance of doing so.

"Couldn't we just go as friends?" he asked.

"Honey, at this level…the press…they don't understand nuance. They will have a field day with us. Oh, what a mess."

She was obviously conflicted about the decision. She wanted to help, but she was afraid it might make things worse.

"I just need one of those passes so I can move about the grounds freely. I will probably spend most of my time away from the box anyway."

"Oh, I see," Harper answered sarcastically. "Not only do you want me to take you, but you are also going to abandon me all day? Some date you are!" Harper was trying hard to hide her fear. She was talking herself into the idea.

"Oh fine! What the hell do I care anyway?" she sighed. "Let the people talk."

"Thank you, Harper. We are almost there. We are going to catch him," Cal spoke reassuringly.

"I'm glad you think so, dear. Just promise me one thing."

"Anything."

"Promise you will help clear my husband's name once all of this is settled. He truly was a good man and he deserves better than the way he has been treated in the papers."

"I will do my best," Cal said.

"Thank you. I will have a Millionaires Row pass overnighted that will get you anywhere in Churchill Downs you want to go. Be careful and do come see me in the box on Saturday."

Cal waited for the click on the other end of the line. He was still standing in the middle of his den with only a towel wrapped around his waist. Across the street, his neighbor was mowing grass and some kids were playing basketball in a driveway.

The rest of the world was enjoying the approach of spring. Meanwhile, Cal was preparing for one of the biggest days of his life.

He placed the phone on its cradle and returned to his bedroom to get dressed.

26

By Thursday afternoon, Cal was ready to venture out of the house to replace the items he had lost in Argentina. Cell phone, driver's license, and gun.

He couldn't stay holed up waiting for Gallo to strike. Besides, he was driving himself crazy thinking about Emma. He wanted to call her. Was she okay? He missed her already and he was concerned about how she was dealing with the experiences of the past week. Twice he picked up the phone and began dialing the number she had given him for her parents' house, but each time he hung up before completing the call. He wanted to give her time to rest. Don't push it.

The MG was exactly where he had left it. He hopped in and placed the key in the ignition. Just as he was about to crank the starter, he had a sudden thought.

He popped the hood and climbed out of the car. Raising the hood, he studied the engine for any sign of tampering. Valves and wires and belts. Everything seemed normal.

Next, he lay down on his back and slid under the car. He searched for any foreign objects that looked out of place on the underbelly of the MG. Still nothing.

Satisfied Gallo had not placed a bomb or tracking device on the vehicle, he returned to the driver's seat and fired up the engine.

He backed out of the driveway. His grass-mowing neighbor had stopped to watch the strange examination Cal had given the car before starting it. He waved to the man as he drove past. His neighbor waved back and watched inquisitively as Cal pulled away.

Cal's first stop was the County Clerk's office on Winchester Road to get the driver's license he would need in order to obtain the other two items on his list.

As he waited in line to have his photo snapped, he kept looking over his shoulder nervously. He was afraid Gallo was watching his every move. He had a sense of impending danger and he felt naked without his phone and weapon. If Gallo was going to attack, Cal was currently at his weakest point.

The driver's license process went off without a hitch, as did the acquisition of a new cell phone. Finally, Cal was starting to feel like a human again. Next stop was the gun shop where he would complete his restocking.

Bells hanging on the back of the gun shop's glass door jingled to announce Cal's entry.

"Hey there, good buddy. What's new?"

Over the years, Cal had forged a friendship with Clint Stevens, the owner of his favorite local gun shop.

Clint sold every gun a man could legally buy. And a few that he couldn't. Once a customer entered Clint's inner circle, he gained access to the back room where, for the right price, he could get his hands on all kinds of unique weapons.

Cal had seen some of Clint's private stock, but he had never before required any firepower that wasn't provided by his trusty .38 semi-automatic.

"How's business?" Cal asked as he closed the shop door behind him.

The bells jingled again as the door clicked shut.

"Oh, can't complain. I can hardly keep guns on the shelf now that everyone is afraid the government is going to ban them. Thank god for those idiot talking heads who scare everyone into stocking up," Clint replied.

"I don't know which is worse," said Cal. "The politicians or the clowns who talk about them all day."

"You got that right. Well, what can I do for you today? How is that .38 working out?"

"Funny you should ask. It's a great gun. In fact, I'm here for another one." Cal thought it was best not to go into detail about the events of his past week.

"Sure, we can do that. It's a classic piece. Always keep a few in stock," replied Clint as he came out from behind the counter and walked toward his stock room in the back of the shop.

He disappeared from sight behind two swinging saloon doors that separated the stock room from the sales floor.

The shop was a small shotgun-style unit tucked away in a strip mall off of Winchester Road. Inside, the walls were lined with dark wood paneling. It looked like the decor hadn't changed since Stevens opened the place back in the seventies.

Three decades of cigarette smoke stained the fiber ceiling tiles. The smoky smell lingered in the showroom even when no was smoking, and it mixed with the leathery smell of gun oil. The odor was similar to an old barber shop.

Shotguns and handguns hung from hooks on the wood-paneled walls. A few clothing racks in the center of the showroom displayed hunting vests and flannel shirts. Mostly safety orange and camo.

A long glass display case formed the outer perimeter of the showroom. It was stocked full of smaller weapons like handguns, knives, and survival kits. The case ran the length of the wall on Cal's right and extended back to the double doors Clint had passed through to access the stock room.

Cal could hear Clint talking in the back of the store as he searched for the requested weapon.

"Say, you talked to Ed lately?" Clint hollered from the stock room. He was referring to their mutual friend Ed Masters from the *Herald-Leader*. "I wanted to ask if he's got any hot tips on the Derby."

"I saw him a few weeks ago, but we didn't talk about the race," Cal answered. "My money is on the favorite, Valkyrie. He is a beautiful horse and rumor has it he has the speed to break Secretariat's record."

Clint whistled as he pushed through the swinging doors.

"No kidding? That speed record has been in place for almost 50 years. I'd like to see that happen."

"Same here. I'm not usually one to bet on the favorite, but this year I think it's a lock."

"Alright then, pal. I'll take your word for it."

Clint handed the .38 to Cal for him to inspect. It felt good in his hand. He pulled back the slide and dropped out the magazine. He examined it and popped it back into the handle.

Cal had a question on his mind. He decided to ask Clint. He leaned forward and lowered his voice.

"Hey, between you and me, do you have anything that would make it through a metal detector?"

Clint didn't blink an eye at the question.

"Maybe. What do you have in mind?"

"I'm dealing with a pretty bad dude right now and I hate to be without a piece, but I am going to an event with a strict no firearms policy."

"Step into my office," Clint said. He walked over to the front door, locked it, and flipped a sign that said OUT TO LUNCH. Then he led Cal back through the swinging doors into the stock room.

"What you're looking for is a gun made entirely of plastic. Completely undetectable by your standard screener."

"A plastic gun, eh? Do they work?"

"Oh yeah. Welcome to the wonderful world of technology."

Clint pulled a case from under the back counter and placed it in front of Cal. He popped the hinges and opened the case, displaying a strange-looking weapon that hardly resembled a traditional firearm.

"This here baby was made on a 3D printer. Not a single piece of metal in it."

"You mean a *computer* generated this weapon and printed it?" Cal couldn't believe his ears.

"Yep. Pretty amazing, right?"

Cal's mind started racing at the implications of a weapon like this one. The technology could be dangerous in the wrong hands.

"Have you sold any of these yet?"

"A couple, but all that is confidential, of course."

"Sure. Wow."

"Give it try. It's amazingly lightweight."

Cal reached into the case and extracted the strange weapon. It reminded him of a rubber band gun he used to play with as a kid. The plastic gun felt like a toy in his hand.

"That is one hell of an odd piece," Cal finally said. "It feels like it's from the future."

"Well, it kind of is," Clint replied. "One day, I will be able to program the exact dimensions of your hand into a computer and custom print a gun made just for you in a matter of minutes. How about that?"

"Pretty amazing stuff."

Cal shook his head and returned the plastic gun to its case. "I have to be honest with you, Clint. I don't know if I'm ready for a change like this one. I think I might stick with my old faithful and take my chances. The .38 has never failed me yet."

Clint nodded with patient understanding.

"No problem, pal. I don't blame you. In fact, I'm a bit of a traditionalist myself. But I couldn't pass up the chance to shoot one of these bad boys once I learned about them."

"I hear you there. Actually I wouldn't mind taking a crack at it some time, if you're offering."

"Of course, my man. Come out to the farm on a Saturday and we'll have a field day with it. I've got a few other beauties out there I think you would like, too."

"Challenge accepted. Listen, Clint, thanks. I always appreciate it."

"Anytime, brother," Clint answered as he rung up the .38 and placed it in a box for Cal.

As Cal left, he unlocked the front door and flipped the window sign back to WE'RE OPEN. He threw a salute to Clint and headed to the car.

The only thing left to do now is buy a new suit. His threadbare tuxedo was somewhere in a Miami landfill. If he was going to be on Millionaires Row, he would need something snazzy. This one is going on the Halcott tab, he chuckled to himself.

Cal wiped the smile from his face and removed the .38 from its box. He loaded the clip and slid the gun under his driver's seat.

27

The next day Cal passed in a state of paranoia, wondering when Gallo would make his move. Every car that drove down his street might be carrying an assassin sent to finish the job that was started in Buenos Aires.

He decided it was best to lay low and venture out of the house as little as possible while he waited for Saturday to come. He kept the .38 loaded on his coffee table just in case. Every few minutes, he crept up to the front window and pulled back the curtain to watch for anything out of the ordinary.

All day, he watched and waited. Nothing happened. No one came to the door. Nothing suspicious occurred.

Had Gallo given up on him? Surely not. Cal had information that could put Gallo away for a long time. He could not allow those secrets to be leaked.

No, the only possible answer was that Gallo was lying in wait for the best opportunity to make his move. A man like Gallo probably has henchmen all over the world who do his bidding. For all Cal knew, Gallo had bought off one of his neighbors. Maybe the guy across the street was reporting Cal's every move.

The paranoia was taking hold. There was no one Cal could trust with the information he had. No proof of his Argentine captivity. Only his word against Gallo's.

With race day rapidly approaching, Cal had to form a plan fast. He knew Gallo's secret and he knew his motive. He even had a pretty good idea about how it would go down. If only he could help the authorities catch Gallo red-handed in the act.

Finally, Saturday arrived. The big day had come. First thing in the morning, Cal called his friend Joe Brand, the ex-cop. He wanted to explain the situation to Brand and get his perspective. Besides, Joe is a good guy to have in his corner when he was working on a case as dangerous as this one.

He picked up his new cell phone and dialed Brand's number.

"This is Brand."

"Hey, Joe. It's Cal. Do you have a minute?"

"Yeah, bud. What's up?"

"Well, do you remember a few weeks back when I called about John Hood?"

"Yep."

"Okay, I'm still working on that case and it has gotten a lot bigger than I imagined it would."

"Is Hood giving you trouble?"

"Not exactly. I'll give it to you straight. Get ready for this one," Cal replied. "I have it on good authority the

Halcott death was no suicide. He was murdered and I heard the murderer's confession with my own ears."

"What? Who confessed?"

"Are you familiar with Augusto Gallo, the famous Argentine horse breeder?"

"I've heard of him."

"He is the guy. I don't have time to explain everything, but the short version is I had a run-in with him last week and he divulged not only that he was behind the murder, but also his motive for it. Apparently, Halcott was standing in the way of his masterplan."

"What is his masterplan?"

"To fix the Kentucky Derby."

"You can't be serious. Why on earth would he confess that to you?"

"Let's just say, at the time, he thought I would not be around to spread the message."

"Cal, what have you gotten yourself into? Have you gone to the police about this yet?"

"Do you think I should?"

"No question. You know I have some gripes with my former employer, but they still work to protect the people of this city. If some Argentine mobster is after you, you need help. This is serious."

"But what if they are colluding with him somehow? Could I be walking right into his hands?"

"Colluding with a crime boss in Argentina? I don't think so, man. You are sounding awfully paranoid right now."

"Maybe I am. I have been feeling pretty skittish lately. I'm not sure who I can trust."

"Listen, Cal. Let me make some calls. I know some people who can help. If you are planning to put a guy like Gallo out of business, you will need backup."

"Fair enough," Cal replied. "I will be at the Derby in a few hours. Gallo will be there and, like I said, he is planning to fix the race. According to his confession, his horse Calavera will post at 50 to 1 odds. I'm not sure how he is going to pull it off, but if he gets his way that longshot is going to be in the Winner's Circle."

"He's going to tamper with the other horses in the field?" Brand asked. "Or is he laying down bribes?"

"I don't know yet. That's why I need to get to the Derby today and investigate."

"When are you leaving?"

"As soon as we hang up."

"Cal, be careful. I am going to alert my contacts in Lexington and Louisville. This is serious and they need to be aware of it. I know of at least two former cops who are working security in Churchill Downs today. At the very least they can watch your back."

"That will work."

Joe had another idea before hanging up. "I'll text you one of their phone numbers in a second. Can't remember it off hand."

"Thanks, Joe."

"Good luck."

When Cal hung up, he felt even less confident than he did before. Joe's concern made him more paranoid than ever. He trusted Joe, but who were Joe's friends? Was there a chance they were in cahoots with Gallo? Could he be walking right into a trap?

He had to take the risk. His own life was on the line as long as Gallo was free. He had no choice but to continue. It was either Gallo or him.

28

As soon as Cal hung up the phone with Joe Brand, he got ready to leave for the Derby. It was 9:00 a.m., and the main event would not start until 6:00, but the tailgating at Churchill Downs had already begun. Cal wanted to get to the track as early as possible so he could start investigating and asking questions.

He donned the brand-new suit he had purchased for the occasion. It was a light grey three-piece complete with a matching Borsalino hat. He polished his shoes and slid them on. The shoes were dark brown, almost a deep reddish color, and they accented his light gray suit.

Cal looked in the mirror and decided he was ready to fit in with the Derby gentry. He ran his fingers along the brim of his hat and slid a gold watch into his vest pocket. The package was complete.

Before walking out the front door, Cal went to the window and did a final survey of the block.

He scanned his yard and the yard of his neighbors. He looked up and down the street for anything out of place. He spotted a few parked cars, examined them closely, looked to see if they had passengers who might be surveilling his property.

Everything was quiet.

Cal locked the front door and headed out to the MG in his driveway. He fired up the engine and set the .38 on the passenger seat. The entry pass Harper had mailed him was tucked into the center console.

Derby day had begun.

As Cal approached the interstate exit for Churchill Downs his excitement kicked into gear.

Even at 11:00 a.m. the traffic on Central Avenue had reached a standstill. Cars were backed up a mile outside the Churchill Downs parking lot. Buses and vans emblazoned with Louisville hotel names shuttled Derby guests back and forth to the track. The shuttles caused as much of the road congestion as the cars.

Cal was overwhelmed by the melee. One of the first things he noticed at his inaugural Derby was the stark contrast between the two groups that intermingled on race day.

On the one hand, there were the rich and famous who spent as much as $50,000 on the spectacle. Even the moderately-priced grandstand and box seats run in the thousands. This side of the Derby patronage was populated by people who wear their best clothes and spare no expense for the special day.

Then there was the other half.

While the rich have designated seats from which to watch the race, everyone else is relegated to the infield where all of the madness transpires.

Cal was familiar with Hunter S. Thompson's gonzo account of the Derby. He had read *The Kentucky Derby is Decadent and Depraved*, and he wondered if he might see some of the debauchery and madness today.

In the infield, not only are there no seats, but there is not even a view of the racetrack. The infield is solely devoted to the party atmosphere that surrounds the main event. Tickets for the infield can be obtained right up until race day at a cost of only about fifty bucks.

Therein lies the stark divide. In the stands, you have people who spend more for their tickets than many of the infield partiers earn in a year.

The mix of people found at the Kentucky Derby is unique, and Cal was witnessing it firsthand. Maybe next year he would try the infield, but this year he was here for business.

Behind Cal in the traffic jam was an $80,000 Audi and in front of him was a pickup truck with three men in the bed who were parading around shirtless. They were slamming beers while dancing in the truck bed and catcalling pedestrians.

Because Churchill Downs was smack in the middle of a residential neighborhood, many of the locals stood in driveways holding signs advertising parking spots for pay. Cal picked a driveway a few blocks from the track and pulled the MG into the spot where he was directed to park.

Before getting out of the car, he grabbed the pass Harper had sent him and looped it around his neck. He looked longingly at the .38. Considering the circumstances, he hated to leave it. But he knew there was no way the weapon would make it past security. Cal quickly placed the gun in the glove box and climbed out of the car.

He handed the guy who parked him a $20.

"What is the best way in?" he asked.

"You see this huge crowd of people?" the guy asked. "Follow 'em."

Thanks a lot, smartass. Cal nodded at the guy and stepped on the sidewalk, where he was quickly swallowed up by the mass of people. They pressed in around him on all sides. The crowd carried him shuffling forward in the direction of the entry gates.

29

Cal finally understood the Derby crowd hype as he approached the entry gates of Churchill Downs. According to his research, about 170,000 people would pass through these turnstiles today. It was barely noon and the gates were backed up all the way to Central Avenue. Cal took his spot in the growing line.

All around him, cars honked in every direction. The crowd multiplied before Cal's eyes. He had never seen so many people attempting to squeeze into one place. The noise was nearly unbearable, as was the invasion of personal space. Cal could not go more than a few seconds without getting bumped by one of the people packed tightly around him.

Cal did his best to block out the irritations and focus on the experience, considering this was his first visit to the Kentucky Derby. He was here investigating Gallo, but he still hoped to take it all in and enjoy himself as much as possible.

Positioned just outside the entry gates of the track was a huge bronze statue of a powerful-looking thoroughbred in full gallop. When Cal got close enough to read the plaque, he learned the horse was a sculpture of 2006 Derby winner Barbaro, whose ashes were buried in the spot where the monument now stood.

In addition to the champion horse's name, the plaque at the base of the statue bore a quote from Eric Liddell, the Olympic sprinter on whose life the film Chariots of Fire was based.

"I believe God made me for a purpose, but He also made me fast. And when I run, I feel His pleasure."

Cal stood before the great statue and admired the horse to whom it was dedicated.

"Excuse me. Will you take our picture?"

The request interrupted Cal's introspection and brought him back into the moment. He turned and saw the man who had asked the question. He was standing with his wife and two kids. In his extended right hand was a camera.

"You just have to line us up and push this button," he was saying as he pointed to the button that would snap the shutter closed and forever commemorate this moment in the family's history.

Cal accepted the camera from the man and waited for them to take their positions at the base of the Barbaro statue.

When they were in place, he raised the camera to his eye and adjusted the viewfinder, so the family was centered below the stallion's massive torso. He counted to three.

"Say 'horse manure,'" he instructed just before clicking the button.

The kids, of course, thought this was hilarious.

"Horse manure!" they shouted, giggling.

"Good one," Cal replied.

He handed the camera back to the father who did not appear to be nearly as amused as the kids were.

"Thanks a lot," the dad muttered and shoved the camera into his pocket as they reclaimed their spot in line.

Cal could see the turnstiles just ahead. He could feel the nerves rising in his stomach. It was partly because he was going to have to play another role in Millionaires Row today. He never enjoyed that aspect of the job, but sometimes it had to be done.

The excitement of the crowd around him added to the nervous tension. The energy buzzing throughout Churchill Downs today was unlike anything Cal had ever felt. The whole place was electric.

But more than anything else, Cal's nerves were coming from the inevitable encounter he knew he would have today with Augusto Gallo. Would Gallo try to take him out? Would he run? Would Cal be able to catch him?

So many unanswerable questions were running through Cal's mind. To make matters even more tense, he still wasn't exactly sure what he was going to do when he ran into Gallo. He was hoping the moment would dictate his actions.

All of these factors combined to form an ever-tightening lump of tension in the pit of Cal's stomach as he stepped closer and closer to the entry gate.

It's not too late to back out, he thought. I could walk away right now. Head back to my car and get the hell out of here. That would be the sane thing to do.

"Pardon me, sir. Why are you standing in this line?" came a sudden voice to his left.

Cal looked at the speaker with confusion in his eyes. She understood he was caught off guard.

"The badge around your neck, sir. You have paid good money to avoid waiting in this line," she continued. "Please come with me and I will take you directly to your seat."

Cal shrugged and followed her. He could feel the eyes of the crowd on him as he skipped the line and waltzed right through the entry gate with no questions asked.

The woman hung a right once inside the gates and led Cal past the paddock where the horses were promenaded for public view before each race.

"You are just in time," she called over her shoulder. "The first post of the day is in about 30 minutes. You are welcome to hang out here if you like. The horses will be in the paddock any minute."

She turned and waited patiently for Cal's response.

"That's okay. I will be down later," he answered. "I'm, uh, I think I am heading for…where's Millionaires Row?"

He did not sound like someone who belonged in that section.

"Yes, of course, sir. We are delighted to have you today. Please let us know if there is anything we can do to make your day more pleasurable. Anything at all."

Cal felt completely out of place. He nodded and continued following her until they reached an elevator. The elevator had no buttons—only a single keyhole on a wall-mounted control panel.

The woman inserted a key into the hole, and, within a few seconds, the elevator doors opened before them.

She placed a forearm on the retracted door to hold it while Cal stepped inside. Then, she reached into the elevator and pressed one of the two glowing buttons.

"This will take you directly up, sir. And remember, let us know if we can do *anything* for you."

She stepped back out of the elevator car. The last thing Cal saw was her exuberant, smiling face as the doors closed shut.

Cal felt the car begin to rise. He took a deep breath and braced himself.

30

The elevator dinged when it reached the top floor and the doors opened on Millionaires Row. Cal was presented with a large dining room full of tables covered in white cloths and topped with fine china. Just inside the door to his right was a long, wooden bar coated with a shiny lacquer. Behind it stood two bartenders in tuxedos waiting to take drink orders.

On the opposite side of the room from the bar was a green row of betting windows, each manned by a Churchill Downs official. These bet-takers were trained to explain the rules of gambling to first-time Derby guests. They wore white button-down shirts and green bowties.

A small line of bettors was forming at each window. Cal deduced one of the day's races was about to begin. The television monitors mounted on all of the walls in the dining room confirmed his suspicion. In flashing white letters, they proclaimed:

TWO MINUTES TO POST

The fourth wall of the room, directly opposite the entryway, was the main focal point of Millionaires Row. The entire wall was made of glass and, through it, Cal could see all of Churchill Downs below. He strolled over to the glass wall to get a better look.

When he reached the window, he saw openings in it that led out to a private observation deck shared by the Millionaires Row attendees. He exited the glass door and stepped on the balcony.

As soon as he was outside, the noise from the crowd filled the air. Cigar smoke and stale beer flooded his nostrils. Directly below him were the grandstands and the box seats. He peered over the edge of the green railing, and he could see the rows of boxes below. People stood shoulder-to-shoulder as far as his eye could see.

Just below the railing was strung a mesh net that extended approximately 18 inches out from the observation deck. The net was designed to catch any dropped items and prevent them from falling six floors on to the heads of the people below. A dropped cell phone would cause a scandal for cracking some poor schlub's skull in the box seats.

Cal continued to explore the track from his bird's eye view. From the observation deck, he had a perfect vantage point of the finish line. He could see the tall pole on the side of the dirt track which indicated the culmination of each race.

He knew a photo was snapped at this pole the instant a horse crosses the invisible line. The Photo Finish.

Inside the circle of dirt spread the vast infield. From the Millionaires Row balcony, Cal could see all of the madness ramping up in the infield. He and his Millionaires Row brethren were like kings presiding over a coliseum of gladiators.

The infield was a writhing mass of revelers. Blankets and tarps were spread out on the grassy field. They were strewn with people at various levels of intoxication from wobbly to fully prostrate. Trash was scattered everywhere. The infield looked like a human landfill.

"Quite a mess out there already, eh?" a man standing next to Cal on the balcony questioned.

"So it appears. Do you think it's worth it?" Cal responded.

"Depends on who you ask I suppose. They say somewhere around 60,000 people will pack in down there at some point today. So I guess it is worth it to some."

"Sixty thousand people will make that a pretty tight spot I would say."

"Indeed it will. I believe I will stay up here," the man replied as he raised a pair of binoculars to his eyes and trained them on a set of starting gates which had been wheeled out to the track in preparation for the upcoming race. Cal followed the man's gaze and squinted to see the start line.

Jockeys and horses were prancing on the track, walking in tight circles by the gates. Some of the horses were jittery and zig zagging uncomfortably as they watched their competitors load into the gates. One by one, each horse was led to its position in the post and coaxed into the chute. The metal door slammed shut behind their flanks, locking them into position.

When the final horse was loaded into the chute, Cal heard the announcer's voice boom through the loudspeaker.

"They're at the post!"

For a split second, all of Churchill Downs was silent as they waited for the race to begin.

Then the bell rang, and the announcer shouted again.

"And they're off!"

The horses broke from the starting gates and the crowd went wild. Everyone cheered for the horse they had bet to win.

Cal watched the horses run around the track. The dirt flew. The hooves thundered. The announcer rattled off the order of each thoroughbred like an auctioneer closing a sale. The enthusiasm of the crowd was intoxicating. Cal could feel the energy coursing through him right down to the last second when the pack of racehorses crossed the finish line directly beneath him. The entire stadium exhaled, and the spectators fell back into their seats.

When the race ended and the cheering subsided, Cal turned to the man with the binoculars.

"How did you do?"

"Not too well on that one," the man sulked. "The damned two horse just lost me three grand."

"Yikes. Better luck next time," Cal replied. He headed back into the dining room to look for Harper.

"There you are, Mr. Diamond! Harper has been looking all over for you today. What took you so long? Where's your mint julep?"

Cal recognized the speaker as a woman from the Bonnycastle party, but he did not recall her name. Before he could answer, she was talking again.

"Follow me. We have a table over here. Have you tried the buffet yet? It is delicious. Some of these stuffy types complain that the food is buffet style, but just wait until you try it. It is gourmet," she drawled the words slowly as she spoke them. "And besides they will make anything for you if you just ask. Did you watch the last race? Looks like it's not a good day for the favorites so far. You would think the experts would be better at their job than that. What beautiful weather we have today though, don't you agree, Mr. Diamond? Not too hot, not too cold."

Cal couldn't manage to squeeze even a word in as the woman spoke with the excitement of "Derby fever." He simply nodded when appropriate and followed her lead to the reserved table.

"Harper, look who I have found!" she exclaimed as she approached the group.

Harper raised her eyes from the table and spotted Cal.

"It's about time! Don't you realize the Kentucky Derby is an all-day event?" Harper winked at Cal as she chastised him.

"After the Bonnycastle party, I wasn't sure if I could keep up. You take your celebrating seriously," Cal answered.

The entire table laughed and raised their glasses in response. Everyone shifted around and made room for another chair to be added next to Harper's.

"Sit down here, Frankie. I'll get us a drink," Harper said as she placed a hand on Cal's shoulder and pressed him into the seat.

She whisked off to the bar, leaving Cal alone with the table full of millionaires.

"Well, what do you think so far, Mr. Diamond?" the man to Cal's right asked. "Harper was telling us this is your first Derby."

"Not bad so far. But then I haven't visited the infield yet."

"Oh my heavens. I wouldn't dare. Those people are animals," replied an older woman with a huge white hat. The hat's brim extended so far that the people on either side of her had to duck when she turned her head.

"Come now, Evelyn, I have heard stories about you in the seventies. Don't act like you haven't tried it," a second woman teased. Then she turned to Cal and whispered loud enough for the table to hear, "Evelyn was something of a hippie!"

"Dear, dear. Another lifetime ago..." was Evelyn's only response.

The table was quiet for a moment of self-reflection. It was as though everyone was reminiscing of a Derby past. Cal broke the silence.

"Hell of a view we have up here anyway."

"Indeed it is," Evelyn's husband replied. "Did you watch the last race? Nothing beats our view of the finish line."

"I did. Truly breathtaking. The energy in this place is palpable," Cal answered. Then he had another thought. "I noticed the favorite did not fare well."

"Nor did they yesterday at Oaks. The odds have belied a few false favorites so far this week."

His wife swung her hat in his direction, causing him to duck to avoid the brim.

"Harold, you just love throwing around your racing terminology. Now tell the young man what you mean."

"The boy's not stupid, Evelyn," Harold answered. He turned back to Cal and spoke.

"A false favorite is a horse that is favored despite being outclassed by other competition in the field. But you already knew that, right, young man?" he asked, winking.

Cal nodded in response.

"So you are saying there is an underdog in the field that is not getting the credit it deserves, and it ends up surprising the competition?"

"That would be one possibility. Or another might simply be everyone bets on the wrong horse and the odds incorrectly tip in its favor. You end up with a favorite that, in all reality, has no chance of winning. I think that is what happened in the last race. The odds were wrong at the post."

"Interesting," Cal responded.

"What's all this about the odds being wrong?" Harper asked as she returned to the table with a drink in each hand. She placed one glass in front of Cal.

"Old-fashioned for you, dear."

"Thank you," Cal replied and took a sip from the bourbon-filled glass.

Harper continued, "Are you all talking about the favorites again? You better quit that. You don't think my Valkyrie is a false, do you?" As she spoke she was looking at Harold. He seemed to be the gambling expert of the group.

"No, dear. I do not. I have been here for over 40 runnings of this race. I saw Secretariat win in '73. Lord knows I will not be here for many more. But I have never been more excited about a horse than I am about yours. If ever there was a chance to break Secretariat's record, it's today."

The rest of the table nodded in agreement. Cal couldn't tell if they were humoring Harper or if they really meant it.

"Track conditions are ideal, too," spoke the third man at the table. "Nice and firm and not a cloud in the sky. The Derby will run fast."

"Oh, I would love to see a speed record! And Harper's horse! Wouldn't that be amazing?" exclaimed the wife of the third man. She was much younger than her husband. Blond and pretty with big...eyes.

"It would be a great win for our farm. And for Sterling," Harper spoke quietly.

Evelyn placed her hand on Harper's shoulder and consoled her. She reached across Harper's lap and touched Cal's arm.

"It's very good of you to escort Harper today. I know she thinks highly of you. And she deserves the best."

Cal nodded solemnly and looked to Harper. She had tears in her eyes. Evelyn removed a tissue from her purse and handed it to her. She took it and dabbed at her eyes.

"Let's get some air," Harper suddenly stated and stood up. She headed for the balcony and Cal followed behind her.

In between races, the observation deck was relatively quiet. There were a few people standing outside when Cal and Harper got there, but the balcony was empty enough to give them some privacy.

As soon as Harper stepped through the doors, she regained her composure and all traces of sadness left her face. Cal wondered if the news media and paparazzi kept cameras trained on the Millionaires Row balcony at all times. He assumed they probably did, which helped explain Harper's abrupt transition.

"What's the plan?" she immediately asked once they were out of earshot. "Have you spotted Gallo yet?"

"I was going to ask you the same question. Do you expect him up here?"

"He usually always is, but I haven't seen him yet. His absence from this observation deck is definitely suspicious. He is here every year."

"He knows we are on to him now. He's laying low. Do you think he is aware I'm here?"

"I haven't told anyone, but it would not surprise me if he knows. There are lots of unfamiliar faces in this room."

"Right. He probably has informants."

"What about the horses? Are they safe? Is Valkyrie safe?"

"I talked to an old friend from the Metro Police Department and he sent a few guys to help me keep an eye on things. They are supposed to have security badges, which will allow them to move around the track freely.

"How will they know what to do?"

"They have been briefed, but I am going to call them here in a second. I would like to get down to the stables and check on the horses. Can I get in?"

"Yes, it shouldn't be a problem with that Millionaires Row pass."

She pointed to the badge around Cal's neck.

"And if anyone gives you any trouble, call me."

"Okay, I'll head down now. What about these folks? Will they wonder why I am leaving already?"

"Don't worry about them. I will handle it. Besides, their eyeballs will be floating in bourbon an hour from now," Harper said.

Cal managed a chuckle at the mental image Harper had conjured. Somehow all behavior gets a pass on Derby day. It's like the Las Vegas slogan. What happens at the Derby stays at the Derby. You wake up Sunday morning and it is a brand-new day. A clean slate for another year in Kentucky.

"Oh, and by the way," Harper was saying, "you might want to avoid the paddock area this afternoon. When the celebrities do their little red-carpet photo shoot, that place will be a madhouse. Or, hey, check it out if you feel like it. It can be fun."

"Good to know. I'm hoping to get some exclusives for my Hollywood insider blog," Cal joked. "When does that happen?"

"You are crazy. I think around 3."

Cal winked as he turned to leave.

"Hey, Cal!" Harper called after him.

Cal looked back at her.

"Take care of my horse!"

"I'm on it."

31

It is amazing what you can do when you have a Millionaires Row pass wrapped around your neck, Cal thought as he flashed the badge to security at the Churchill Downs stables.

The security guards smiled and stepped to the side to welcome him. They unclipped the velvet rope and pointed in the direction of Valkyrie's stable.

Cal looked at his pocket watch and saw it was 2:00 p.m. A little over four hours until the big race. Plenty of time to talk with Harper's jockey Kyna Ryan. He hoped Kyna and the other jockeys would have some information about Augusto Gallo and his men. Cal figured if anyone had insight on potential foul play, it would be the people who work with the horses several hours each day.

Just inside the security line, Cal stopped and removed his cell phone from his pocket. He dialed the phone number Joe Brand had given him and waited for his security backup to answer.

"Hello."

"Are you Brand's guy?"

"Yes."

"Can you come to the back stables? I have a job for you."

"Yes."

"Find Valkyrie's stable and meet me there."

"10-4."

A man of few words, Cal thought as he hung up the phone. Oh well, I'm not hiring him for his conversation. If Joe trusts him, then he is good enough for me.

As Cal strolled through the back stables, he could feel the excitement in the air. This was the biggest day of the year for everyone working behind the scenes, and for some, the most important day of their lives. Trainers, veterinarians, owners, farriers, stable hands, and jockeys all milled about. The place was abuzz with anticipation.

Cal spotted Kyna Ryan in front of one of the stables and headed in her direction. He recognized her from his visit to Halcott Farms the first time he saw Valkyrie.

As he approached, Kyna was leaning forward into the top half of a split door that opened into a wooden stable. The bottom half of the door was closed and Kyna was resting her elbows on it as she leaned into the stall. The upper half of her body disappeared into the darkness of the stall. From the outside, the stall's occupant was hidden from view, but a brass nameplate over the door proclaimed it was the Derby favorite Valkyrie.

Straw protruded from the bottom of the stall door. The earthy musk of the dry straw mixed in the air with the pungent aroma of fresh manure. The strong smell singed

Cal's nostrils, but it wasn't a bad one. It was the healthy scent of a farm.

When he got close to the stall, Cal heard Kyna talking softly to the horse inside. Her voice was almost a whisper as she spoke soothingly to the animal in her lilting Irish accent.

"Today is the day, baby. Today is the day you make history," she was saying.

Cal was only a few feet away when he stepped on the straw and it crunched under his foot.

When Kyna noticed Cal's presence, she stopped talking and dropped back out of the stall. As she did, the horse inside reared its head and whinnied. His long nose extended out the open stall door next to Kyna. They both stood facing their guest.

Cal froze in the presence of the regal horse. He was in awe of Valkyrie all over again. The same feelings he had the first time he saw the thoroughbred rushed back. The horse snorted and bobbed, pawing at the straw inside its stall. The head was completely black, shiny even, except for the single white patch on the bridge of his nose.

Valkyrie's charisma was captivating. It was impossible to ignore the magnetism he exuded. He commanded respect and adoration, and Cal could not help but award it each time he saw the horse.

Kyna broke the silence.

"Can I help ye, sir?"

Cal snapped out of his trance and looked at the jockey who had just spoken. She, too, had a fire in her eyes that mimicked Valkyrie's. Her glowing eyes and stiff posture announced she did not take flak from anybody. She had to be tough to make it to this level.

As he returned to reality, Cal realized Kyna did not recognize him. She glanced down at the Millionaires Row badge around his neck as she waited for him to respond.

"You're Kyna Ryan, right?"

"I am."

She spoke with confidence, and her voice held a note of suspicion. Cal decided to be completely honest with her. She was the closest he would get to an inside person, and he knew his investigation depended on insight from the jockeys.

"I thought I recognized you," he replied. He extended his hand for a shake.

"My name is Cal Tyson. I am a friend of Harper's."

Kyna took his hand and shook it but gave no response. Valkyrie neighed slightly at the sudden move and encroachment by a stranger. Kyna turned and stroked his nose, whispering softly to him.

"I don't want to take up too much of your time on a day like this, so I am going to come right out with it."

"Okay," Kyna responded with a look of confusion in her eyes.

"Have you noticed any strange activity down here at the stables? Any unusual characters wandering around or causing trouble?"

"Do you mean other than you?" she shot back at him, again eyeing the Millionaires Row badge which rested over his suit coat.

Cal realized then he had not explained anything to her. No wonder she was combative.

"You're right. Let me start over," he breathed and then began again.

"We have a mutual employer. Harper Halcott. I am a private investigator in Lexington, and she hired me to investigate the death of her husband," Cal explained. "You and I have briefly met once at the Halcott Estate when John Hood was showing me around the property."

As Cal spoke, he lowered his voice and looked over his shoulder to make sure they weren't being watched.

"Over the course of the past month, I have been gathering clues and narrowing down suspects. And I have arrived at a conclusion, which is why I'm here now. I believe Sterling's death is related to an ongoing attempt to affect the outcome of the Derby. Someone is going to try and tamper with the race today. So I am down here hoping to uncover some clues. That's why I'm wondering if you have seen any suspicious characters today."

As Cal spoke, Kyna's eyes grew wider. When Cal finished explaining, she motioned for him to come closer. She turned her back and assumed the position she had previously occupied with her elbows on the stall facing inward through the open top door. Unspeaking and with her back to Cal, she waited.

Cal got the idea and leaned in next to her, so both were facing into the darkness of the stall. Valkyrie's head bobbed between them. Cal could smell the sweetness of the horse's flesh mixed with sweat, hay, and manure. He waited for Kyna to answer.

When she spoke, she was quiet, almost whispering.

"It might be nothing, but I actually have noticed something suspicious happening today."

Cal turned to face her and listened intently.

"On a big race day like this, we sometimes see unknown faces wandering around the stables. Media, celebrities, and such. The thing is they usually know their boundaries. They ask questions or take photographs, but they never get too close to us or the horses. It's kind of an unspoken rule that you respect the athletes and you don't harass anyone before an event."

Cal nodded in acknowledgement.

"Well, this morning we had a guy down here who identified himself as a track veterinarian. He had all the credentials, but none of the jockeys had ever seen him before. The guy was convincing. He said he was running some race day tests to make sure the horses were ready to run."

"Did you let him examine Valkyrie?"

"Absolutely not," Kyna responded with pride. "Not a soul in this stadium is going to touch my horse unless Ms. Halcott herself walks down here with him."

"Good. And the other jockeys? Did they permit this veterinarian to touch the horses?"

"Some did. I saw it. You have to remember we don't have a lot of power down here. If we think an owner or a trainer orders a change, we have to go along with it—even if we disagree. It's not up to us. I'm just lucky I know the Halcotts well. Ms. Halcott gives me a lot of autonomy with Valkyrie. Anyhow, I had a bad feeling about the guy, so I told him we have our own vet and he was doing just fine."

"How did he respond to that?"

"He got mouthy. Said he could disqualify a horse if he wanted to, so I better not give him any trouble. I told him to go talk to Ms. Halcott if he wanted, but until then, he wasn't touching my horse."

Cal nodded.

"This is all beginning to make sense," he said.

"Do you think it's related to your investigation?"

"Yes. I have reason to believe there is a plan afoot to tamper with the horses in order to put a longshot in the

Winner's Circle. And what better way to do it than to— "

"Drug the favorites?!" Kyna exclaimed. "Oh no, surely not!"

Kyna was in disbelief at the thought of tampering with the most respected event in horse racing.

"What monster is behind this?"

Cal paused for a moment before responding. On the one hand, he hated to add to the nerves Kyna was no doubt feeling already. But, then again, the more knowledge she had about the plot, the better she could fight it. And she might also become a valuable asset in the investigation if she could be on the lookout for clues.

"It is Augusto Gallo."

Kyna's jaw dropped. She was in shock at the revelation.

"Why would he…" she trailed off. She couldn't find the words.

"I don't know what possesses a person to do something like this," Cal replied. "But I know he is doing it. And now I'm trying to catch him in the act to stop him once and for all."

"I can't believe it. He has to be stopped. What can I do to help?"

"Here. This is my cell phone number. Let me know if you spot the vet around here again. And don't let anyone near Valkyrie."

She took the card he handed her and nodded.

Just at that moment, Brand's man approached Valkyrie's stable.

"Hello, are you Tyson?" he asked.

"Yes. I take it you're Brand's guy. Thanks for your help today."

The guy nodded and waited for his orders. He wore mirror tint aviator sunglasses that hid his eyes and a brown sport coat over a black polo shirt. His lower half was clad with jeans and a pair of dark brown cowboy boots. The cut of his jacket was loose enough to hide his shoulder holster, but Cal's trained eye could barely distinguish the bulge where his pistol was stashed. At least one of us is packing, Cal thought.

"I need you to hang out down here until the race starts and keep an eye on things. Apparently, the target has already made a play at the horses. He hasn't gotten to Valkyrie yet, but he will almost certainly try again. Don't let anyone near this horse unless Kyna here says it's okay."

"Understood."

"Kyna, you and Valkyrie should be safe now."

"That's good. Thank you. But what about the other horses? Have they been drugged?" she asked.

"I'm afraid they may have been."

"We have to tell the owners. We can't let them race. What if they get hurt?"

Cal had no response. He didn't know what to say that would make this situation any better. He looked into Kyna's eyes and saw her concern. He placed his hand on her shoulder.

"We are going to get him. He's going to pay for this. Believe me."

Kyna's eyes flashed and her jaw clenched tightly.

"How can he do this to us?" she growled. "The whole world is watching. A scandal like this could ruin our sport. And the horses! The poor horses."

Kyna's emotion was contagious. Cal felt the hair raise on the back of his neck at her passionate plea. He blinked hard and a surge of anger flowed through him.

"Leave Gallo to me. I have a plan to catch him," Cal soothed, although he wasn't quite sure what that plan was yet. "The best thing you can do today is ride Valkyrie with everything you've got. Put on a performance that will overshadow everything else and show Gallo he was stupid to think he could change history."

Valkyrie recognized his name and snorted. He leaned his huge head toward Kyna and nuzzled her face with his long snout.

Kyna stroked his nose for a few seconds before responding to Cal.

"Nothing can stop this horse from winning today. It's his destiny. I knew it the first time I rode him and it's as true now as it was then."

"Good. I look forward to seeing it happen. I know you will both be great out there."

"Thank you, Mr. Tyson."

Cal gave Valkyrie a final pat on the jowl before walking away. As he headed for the exit that led back to the grandstands, he pondered what he had just heard.

It was becoming abundantly clear Gallo was going through with his plot. Cal knew they should get the horses tested for drugs in their system, but he was afraid Gallo had already thought of that. Whatever cocktail he used was likely undetectable by the routine drug test administered to all of the horses on race day.

Besides, it would take more than a drug test to prove Gallo's connection. The fact he thinks he can manipulate the results of the Derby in broad daylight with millions of people watching demonstrates a level of cockiness Cal had never seen before. There had to be some way he could use Gallo's brashness against him.

32

On the way back from the stables, Cal crossed the paddock to get to the grandstands. He planned to cut through the reserved seating and survey the box seats on his return to Millionaires Row. As he walked, he removed his notepad from his back pocket and jotted down thoughts from the conversation he had just had with Kyna.

- *Suspicious vet in back stables*
- *Drug test horses?*

As soon as Cal entered the paddock, he realized the place had changed dramatically since this morning.

It was a little after 3:00 p.m. and Churchill Downs was bursting at the seams. Over 170,000 people were crowded into the stadium and it looked like most of them were gathered in the paddock Cal was now attempting to cross.

Cal darted to the right to cut around the wave of traffic. No luck. Back to the left. He tried to slip past an elderly couple that had stopped to rest, but he was quickly cut off by a group of middle-aged women in feathered derby hats. There was no easy route across the densely packed paddock.

He spotted a green metal fence on the edge of the crowd. With his left-hand Cal reached across the flow of traffic. He grabbed the fence and reeled himself in out of the current. He leaned against the fence to catch his breath.

An usher who looked to be about 90 years old was also leaning against the fence where Cal had landed. The man smiled and watched the people swarm past. He was completely at ease among the melee.

"Easy does it there, son. Do you know where you are?" the usher leaned into Cal's ear so his voice could be heard over the din of the crowd.

Cal hadn't quite recovered yet. He nodded weakly.

"You are right smack in the middle of the action," the man continued. "This here is the paddock. It's where the horses are shown before each race. About twenty minutes prior to post time, the horses are led around a small track in the paddock where bettors can observe them."

The usher paused to give Cal a chance to ask questions. Cal stayed quiet.

"Why, you see everything from here, young fella. That's why I always ask for this job. The most excitement I see all year. The people, they cram against the fence to get a look at the horses. They are looking for any sign that might indicate they are worthy of a bet."

"How many years have you worked the Derby?" Cal began to make conversation since it was clear they were temporarily trapped.

The old-timer didn't hear Cal's question. He was wrapped up in his story.

"Does the horse seem to be limping? Are its legs wrapped? Is it wearing blinkers? How strong does it look? Is it nervous? Are there any gray horses? Did the animal take a dump?" The old man chuckled to himself. "Yep, these are all questions that might be asked from the observation deck of the paddock. Gamblers are looking for any reason to bet or not to bet on a particular racehorse.

"Does anyone get close enough to touch the horses?" Cal asked.

The old man was lost in revelry.

"I say does anyone touch the horses out here?" Cal repeated a little louder.

The old man started out of his daydream. He turned back to Cal.

"Touch them? Oh, no I don't suppose. But then most of them don't even come down here for the horses. The people-watching is more important at the Derby than watching the races themselves!" the man exclaimed. His voice cracked and he began coughing. He raised a silk handkerchief to his mouth and cleared his throat violently. He finally caught his breath and continued.

"Those who enter the paddock's show track must hold a special pass. These passes go only to the thoroughbred owners, along with their immediate family and friends. Only a select few are granted access to the inner circle. Not only are they idolized by tens of thousands at the track, but they also appear on millions of television sets around the world standing next to their prized horses and jockeys. These are the people who own the million-dollar thoroughbreds. To the horse racing industry, they are celebrities."

Time was slipping away. Cal had to keep moving. He patted the old-timer on the shoulder and surged back into the crowd. It was like shoving a kayak into class five rapids. The crowd immediately closed around him and carried Cal forward. He turned and saw the old man disappearing behind him.

The usher smiled as Cal was swallowed up. The old man cupped his hands and shouted a ghostly warning over the roar, "Don't trust the favorite…"

The sea of people swept shut. Cal could only see a few feet in front of him now. He slowly worked his way through the masses. The afternoon sun was high. It warmed the paddock and mixed with the body heat from thousands of spectators.

The stink of the crowd slapped Cal in the face. A mixture of sweat, stale beer, cigar smoke, and vomit. Even with the occasional waft of perfume, it was not a place Cal wanted to linger for long. But he had no choice other than to move with the pulse of the crowd. It had swarmed shut behind him and swallowed him into it. Now all he could do was pass one person at a time as they leaned forward to shout at a friend or raised an arm to take a photo. The crowd was woven together so tightly Cal could not even reach his back pocket to put away his notepad. He was forced to continue carrying it. One move at a time, Cal made his way toward the other side of the paddock.

As he neared the walking track, Cal spotted the source of the congestion. It was not a pre-race showing.

This time, the commotion was happening right next to the show track. An area of the paddock was sectioned off with velvet ropes. Large, muscle-bound security guards with earpieces surrounded the section and they were forcefully removing anyone who came too close.

It was the celebrity photo shoot Harper had told him about!

"I didn't plan this well," Cal muttered.

A large rectangular red carpet had been rolled out and a section of the paddock was designated off limits to regular Derby goers. The roped section included a stretch of carpet that extended to a private exit which led directly up to The Mansion, the most elite clubhouse of Millionaires Row. This allowed celebrities to enter and exit the red carpet without the risk of interacting with the commoners.

Cal had now worked his way close enough to the red carpet to see the show. Cameras were flashing all around him as one celebrity after the next strutted down the carpet and did a lap around the red rectangle. Some waved to the crowd, some signed autographs, others simply postured rebelliously in dark sunglasses and exited as soon as possible.

As he watched, Cal could not help noticing the similarity between the red-carpet show and the procession of the thoroughbreds before each race. These celebrities were being trotted out by their handlers and shown off to the ravenous public who were asking practically the same questions they did about the horses.

Cal smiled, remembering the words of the old usher. He wondered whether people analyzed a celebrity's bowel movements like they do with the thoroughbreds. The sad thing is they probably do.

As he neared the red carpet, Cal suddenly became caught in a surge of the crowd from which he could not escape. He was jostled directly toward the velvet rope and the line of mean-mugging security guards, but he could not stop the wave that carried him from behind.

He would have been thrust on the carpet himself if security had not caught him with an outstretched arm. Cal looked up and attempted to catch his breath. As he did, he realized he was staring directly into the face of Michael Douglas.

"Hi there, young man. Sure, no problem," Douglas said as he took Cal's notepad and pen. He scrawled his signature on the page and handed it back to Cal.

Cal was caught off guard to say the least. He accepted his notepad and pen back from Douglas.

"Um, thanks. You were great in *Falling Down*," he managed to stammer.

Douglas laughed. "It was a fun role to play. A crowd like this one makes a man want to 'fall down', eh, pal?"

Cal gulped and nodded affirmatively. And then Douglas was gone, off to sign another autograph.

Cal opened his notepad to the page Douglas had just signed. Sure enough, there was his autograph.

This day just keeps getting weirder, he thought.

He spotted an opening along the edge of the velvet rope and made a beeline for it. Within a few minutes, he had hit the outer edge of the paddock where a large corridor marked GRANDSTANDS led him trackside. He took the passageway and left the madness of the paddock behind him.

The boxes of the grandstands were filled with the *normal* millionaires. Lawyers and doctors—those who don't quite qualify for Millionaires Row, but who still have ten grand to drop each year on reserved seats. Anywhere else, these people would be the richest in the room, but here at the Derby, they blend into the crowd. Even their expensive suits and elaborate Derby hats fail to distinguish them from the occupants of the adjacent boxes. At the Kentucky Derby, millionaires are commonplace.

Cal scanned the boxes as he walked, wondering if he might see Ed Masters. He knew sometimes Ed and his group of friends would chip in together to reserve a box, each contributing $1,000 or so to meet the minimum purchase price.

As he rounded a large green pole, he abruptly spotted a face he recognized. The face belonged to someone he did not expect to see today, and it caught him off guard. It was Emma.

The instant he saw her, Cal's heart jumped in his chest. She was in a box with a few other people. A distinguished-looking couple in their fifties was seated next to Emma. The woman was fanning herself with a program. Cal guessed they were Emma's parents.

In addition to her parents, Cal noticed a few more people in the box. Another youngish couple was standing and pointing toward the track, and a well-coifed man with a razor-sharp jawline occupied the final seat next to Emma.

As Cal neared her box, Emma stared straight ahead, watching the track. Cal decided to get her attention and say hi. They had not spoken since returning from Argentina and he wanted to know how she was doing.

He walked up behind the box and tapped her on the shoulder.

When she turned to look at him, she was smiling. But the smile quickly faded when she recognized her visitor. The sudden change in demeanor shook Cal a little, but he continued.

"Hi there," Cal said quietly.

No one else in the box had noticed his presence yet.

"Hi," she replied. She looked around at the rest of the box nervously.

"I didn't realize you were coming today. Are these your parents?"

"Um, well, I didn't either. It was a last-minute decision and I was already in Louisville," she stammered. "Yes, these are my parents. And also my sister and her fiancé."

"I see."

Cal was beginning to get the idea something was wrong. He nodded at the sixth occupant of the box.

"Friend of yours?" he asked.

Emma dropped her eyes.

"Yes. A friend of the family," was all she said, but Cal understood.

At this point, Emma's mother turned around and greeted Cal.

"Hello there, young man." She smiled and looked at her daughter. "Are you going to introduce us to your friend, Emma?"

Emma's mother spoke with a polished southern drawl like one who comes from old money.

"This is Cal. We're, um, he is a friend from Lexington."

Cal winced slightly at the dispassionate description of their relationship, but he took it in stride.

"You have a lovely daughter, ma'am. I can't count how many times she has saved my skin."

"Oh?" Emma's mother replied inquisitively.

"It's true. You see, I work for a law firm in downtown Lexington and I am in the library archives every day researching briefs. Thanks to Emma, I always find what I am looking for."

He stole a quick glance in Emma's direction. She was blushing and seemed uncomfortable.

"Oh! Very glad to hear it, Mr.....?"

"Samson. Vic Samson," Cal replied. "Well, I just happened to spot a friendly face and I wanted to say hello. I had better get back to my seat. Good luck."

He spoke the last two words directly to Emma. She was looking right into his eyes, silently pleading for understanding.

"Indeed, Mr. Samson. Do enjoy this beautiful day!" Emma's mother proclaimed and then she turned back to her husband whose eyes had hardly left the track during Cal's visit to the box.

Cal rested his hand on Emma's forearm and squeezed. She placed her hand on top of his and held it. Cal slowly pulled his hand away from her arm. As he withdrew, her hand slid off of his and dropped to her lap. Then, he broke their mutual gaze and fell into the current of the crowd.

After a few paces, he glanced back over his shoulder. Emma had both hands in her lap with her head tilted down. The family friend was staring at Cal aggressively, watching his departure.

33

"Darling, where on earth have you been? You have left us alone up here all day and you've nearly missed the singing of the national anthem."

Harper swept across the floor to Cal as soon as he entered the private room on Millionaires Row. She was carrying one of the track's signature silver cups which indicated its contents was a mint julep. Cal could smell the bourbon on her breath when she reached him and took his arm. The festivities had clearly continued in his absence.

"How did it go down at the stables? Any updates?" She dropped the accent and Southern belle affectation once she was close enough to Cal to lower her voice.

"The good news is you've got a good jockey," Cal replied.

"Tell me something I don't know. I love Kyna. So did Sterling." Her voice trailed off as she mentioned the name of her late husband. "Did you speak with her then?"

"Yes, and she said there was a strange man snooping around the stables today. He apparently identified himself as a track veterinarian and he was asking to examine all of the Derby horses."

"Oh no. We have our own vet. I wouldn't think of allowing a stranger near Valkyrie today."

"Exactly what Kyna said. She refused to let him in without express permission from you."

"Good girl. But what do you think this means?"

"I am afraid we have to expect the worst. It seems Gallo is carrying out his scheme to drug his competitors in order to gain an edge for his longshot Calavera."

"How could he get away with it? Surely any drug would show up in the pre-race blood screen?"

"One would think. My guess is Gallo has some special cocktail that is undetectable. Otherwise, his plot would be too obvious."

"This is just terrible. Should we alert the authorities? We have to stop him."

"The problem is we have no proof yet. There is no way we can convince Churchill Downs to delay the Derby and open an investigation strictly on a hunch."

"I see," Harper acknowledged. She was distraught. "Well, what can we do? Is Valkyrie safe?"

"Valkyrie is in good hands with Kyna. I also stationed a security guard right outside of his stable for the rest of the day. He will be fine," Cal assured her. "Have you seen Gallo up here yet?"

As he spoke, Cal surveyed the room for Gallo and his men.

"Still no sign of him."

"Doesn't surprise me. Well, we should be on the lookout."

Just then, the loudspeaker cut in and rang throughout the stadium.

"Ladies and gentlemen, please stand and join us for the singing of our national anthem!"

All talking in the room ceased and everyone set down their drinks and headed out on the balcony to observe the solemn moment. Harper took Cal's arm and pulled him outside with the rest of the millionaires.

As Cal stood on the observation deck looking out across the stadium, he could see all of Churchill Downs. The grandstands below him, the freshly combed dirt track, and across it, the infield jammed with tens of thousands of revelers who, at this point in the day, were reeling drunk and barely clutching at a semblance of humanity.

The crowd was silent as the words of the Star-Spangled Banner echoed through the stands. Even the raucous infield had paused in deference. Everyone faced the center of Churchill Downs where the American flag was gently blowing in the breeze. Nearly 200,000 people stone-faced and silent, all focused in one direction.

When the performance ended, a huge cheer swelled up across the grandstands and infield. The track radiated with thunderous applause and shrill whistles.

Cal withdrew his pocket watch and checked the time. 5:15. One hour until post.

"It's time!" Harper exclaimed as they reentered the dining room after the national anthem.

"Time for what?" Cal asked.

"Oh, you'll see. Trust me—you are going to like this. It is a once in a lifetime experience, dear! Now come with me."

Again, she was pulling Cal's arm in her direction, coaxing him to follow her. Cal was starting to wonder if Sterling's left arm was longer than his right from all his wife's pulling. Admittedly a tasteless joke, but he couldn't help smiling at the thought.

"Come, come!" Harper entreated.

Cal gave in and followed her out of the dining room. She led him to a private elevator reserved exclusively for Millionaires Row guests. They entered and Harper punched the button labeled TRACKSIDE.

Cal looked at Harper inquisitively, but she gave no response. She only raised her eyebrows and smiled. She was up to something.

The elevator reached the ground floor with a ding and the doors opened to a row of electric golf carts. A few men dressed in suits with earpieces were standing around waiting for orders. They resembled Secret Service agents, and Cal guessed they were hired expressly to serve the rich and famous attendees.

"Hello, Ms. Halcott. Ready for the walkover?"

"We are. This is a friend who will be joining me for support in Sterling's absence."

Cal was always amazed by Harper's poise when discussing the death of her husband. It had been less than two months since he was laid to rest.

"Yes, ma'am. I am honored to be your escort," the security guard answered.

Harper and Cal climbed on one of the golf carts, and the driver zipped through the corridor and out into the exterior grounds of the track.

"Where exactly are we heading?" Cal asked as they sped around the outside perimeter of Churchill Downs.

"You'll see."

Cal realized asking questions was not doing him any good, so he resolved to ride in silence and play Harper's game.

The golf cart bounced along through the back stable area, swerving to avoid temporary barriers and the occasional drunken pedestrian. Eventually, they reached an opening in the track wall similar to the one they had exited. It was a back entrance and it was heavily guarded by security.

They neared the entrance and a guard waved to their driver. He lifted the temporary barrier to the side for the golf cart to enter. They rode through the checkpoint and followed the short access road leading up to the track. Once they passed security, Cal could see the grandstands he had just left.

The view of the grandstands from the back of the track was surreal. It was amazing to see so many people packed into such a small space. A tremendous logistical feat and a testament to all of the planning that goes into pulling off this event each year.

The fence surrounding the track had an opening cut in it that allowed direct access to the dirt from the stables. As they approached the break in the fence the track loomed large like a gigantic movie screen to which they had front row seats.

Cal's head was on a swivel as he took in the view with incredulity.

"Look at all the people," was the only comment he could manage.

Harper smiled. "Yeah, and they are all waiting for us."

"Huh?" Cal asked.

The golf cart skidded to a stop right next to the track rail. Cal and Harper climbed out and joined the small group of people already waiting by the track.

"What is this?" Cal asked.

"This is the walkover," Harper replied. "Kind of like a parade. We are about to take a casual stroll in front of 16 million people. Might want to straighten up your tie. No pressure," she laughed.

Before he could ask for clarification, the Derby horses began to approach via the access road behind him. The jockeys rode atop them in full regalia, adorned with the bright colors of the horses they represent.

Each horse strutted on to the track one by one, followed by its entourage of owners and family. They walked single file in the order of the post position they had drawn for the main event. Valkyrie had post number 3 and, draped across his midsection, was a white tapestry with the numeral emblazoned on it in black lettering.

Cal and Harper watched the procession and awaited their thoroughbred's imminent arrival.

And suddenly there he was next to them. He exited the access road with Kyna Ryan straddling his back. She bounced slightly with each step. Valkyrie even walked like a winner. He exuded pride and confidence. Cal wondered if the horse knew the importance of the race he was about to run.

Kyna nodded and greeted Harper as she passed. Valkyrie was so tall Cal's head was barely level with Kyna's muddy riding boot. He and Harper fell into step next to the Derby favorite. They began walking the quarter mile stretch around the track back toward the cheering crowd.

The second Cal's shoes hit the soft dirt his excitement level increased one hundredfold. He had seen the walkover on television dozens of times. Never in his wildest dreams did he imagine he would one day be a part of it.

He stole a glance at Harper and saw she was as focused and poised as her racehorse. Both seemed to be acutely aware of the historical moment they were living. Cal was standing right next to The Kentucky Derby *favorite* and the horse was just minutes away from the biggest race of his life.

The dirt felt good under Cal's feet. It was soft and spongy on top, so each step left a footprint behind as they walked. Beneath the surface of the top layer was a tightly packed base that had come from weeks of soaking and draining the soil. The ground they were walking on was the most manicured and important dirt on earth.

After fifty or so yards, Harper leaned over and spoke quietly to Cal as they walked.

"Oh, by the way, don't look now, but guess who drew post position 4?"

Cal didn't have to turn around to know Gallo was behind him. The man who had tried to murder him earlier this week—and who was by his own admission attempting to fix the Derby—was now strolling only a few feet away.

Cal turned and looked over his shoulder.

There was Gallo, waving to the crowd as he moved. He was pretending like nothing was amiss. Cal's glance backward caught Gallo's attention. Gallo pivoted his head to confront his rival. The two men stared at each other intensely. Only about twenty feet of dirt separated them.

"I'll catch up with you in a second," Cal said to Harper. "Let's make this interesting," he muttered.

He stopped advancing on the track. Harper and her horse continued moving forward. Within seconds, a surprised Augusto Gallo had overtaken him. Cal started walking again, shoulder to shoulder with Gallo.

"What the fuck do you think you are doing?" Gallo seethed when he and Cal were side by side.

Cal flashed a fake smile and spoke through clenched teeth, "You better play nice. The whole world is watching."

He glanced up at the massive monitor in the infield and, sure enough, he and Gallo were being projected on the screen for millions to see. Cal nodded at the monitor and Gallo turned his head to see.

As soon as Gallo realized they were on camera, he smiled broadly and extended his hand as though he and Cal were old friends.

Cal took his hand and shook it. To those watching at home, it appeared the two were wishing each other good luck in the day's big race. But on the track, the meeting was much grimmer.

"Here's what is going to happen," Cal was saying. "You are going to pull your horse from the race and confess to everything you have done. If you cooperate, this will go smoothly. You might even get out of prison before you die."

"You stupid gringo. I gave you a chance to keep your mouth shut. You could have walked away. You have squandered that chance. Now you will be dead before the post."

Cal paused for a second and considered how he should respond to this threat.

"I see you have chosen the hard way. I assure you if you go through with this plan, not only will you rot in prison, but your family name will be forever tarnished. I will make sure of it."

"We shall see, Mr. Tyson. We shall see," Gallo continued speaking through gritted teeth. He still wore a fake smile. "You will be sorry. And so will that red-headed bitch who hired you." He jerked his head in Harper's direction.

Harper was still about twenty paces ahead of them, walking alongside her thoroughbred. She stole a glance backward and frantically summoned Cal with her eyes.

Cal turned to Gallo one final time and slapped him on the back firmly as he spoke.

"May the best horse win."

Gallo clenched his jaw and spat into the dirt.

Cal increased his pace and caught up with Harper just as she was about to exit the track. When he reached her, Kyna was pulling Valkyrie around for another pass. With only twenty minutes until post, the racehorses would remain on the track until it was time to run.

Kyna was stoic. Completely in the zone. All of her training prepared her for this moment. Before she turned Valkyrie toward the starting gates, Cal signaled for her attention and she paused to wait for him.

"How did it go back there? Did you see the fake vet again?"

"Yes! He walked past twice more, but your security guard scared him off. He never approached the stable again after that."

"Good," Cal replied. "How is Valkyrie? Is he ready?"

"He was born ready."

"And you? How do you feel?"

"I'm ready."

She spoke with confidence, but there was no denying her nerves. Cal could see it in her eyes.

"Don't worry. Everything is under control," Cal lied.

He wished it were true, but the last thing Kyna needed right now was more stress. He patted Valkyrie's shoulder and looked up at Kyna.

"Go get 'em."

Valkyrie pawed at the ground and snorted. Kyna looked back at Cal and Harper once more before allowing the horse to trot back into the center of the track.

Gallo's horse Calavera had already returned to the track with his jockey. Cal looked in the direction of the private trackside area reserved for owners. He was searching the group for Gallo.

He scanned the crowd until he spotted the black suit jacket and slicked hair he knew belonged to Gallo. The Argentine had already exited the dirt track and he was talking excitedly to someone whose countenance was hidden from Cal. Keeping a close eye on Gallo, Cal stepped through the open security door which led off the track.

Suddenly, Gallo turned and pointed directly at Cal and Harper. When he did, the identity of Gallo's conversant was revealed. Cal froze in his tracks. It was the man in the grey suit!

Cal couldn't believe he had failed to connect the dots between his grey-suited stalker and the other man who had been trying to kill him. They had been on to him the entire time since his first meeting with Emma in Lexington!

Even from this distance, Cal could recognize the man's face. He wore his signature suit and a grey fedora pulled low to obscure his scarred face.

When Gallo pointed, the man raised his head to follow Gallo's finger. His missing eye was covered with a black eyepatch. Cal could see the scar extending above and below it. The man's good eye focused on Cal and stared straight at him with a burning intensity.

Cal broke their eye contact and ushered Harper away from the owner's box.

"Cal, did you see that guy with the eyepatch? He is freaking me out. He won't stop staring." Harper was on the verge of panic.

Cal looked back to the spot where he had just seen Gallo and his one-eyed lackey. They were gone. He frantically surveyed the tightly packed crowd between them and the owner's box. There were maybe one hundred feet separating them.

A few feet outside of the owner's box, Cal spotted the grey fedora. Gallo's thug was threading through the crowd, heading right toward them! In just a few seconds, they would be within his grasp.

At that moment, the crisp sound of a bugle rang through the air. The bugler stood on the track directly in front of them, playing the signature "Call to Post" which indicated they were only 15 minutes to the start of the race.

As soon as the bugle sounded, the crowd sucked in toward the rails like a saturated sponge. Any crack between the people was immediately filled as the audience tightened in preparation for the historic rendition of "My Old Kentucky Home" which precedes every Kentucky Derby.

Cal and Harper had nowhere to go. They were frozen in place with people pressed in on all sides. Luckily for them, the man in the grey suit was also stuck. He was almost close enough to reach out and touch them, but he couldn't advance another inch until the crowd subsided. He glowered at Cal and cursed under his breath.

The bugler finished his call to post and lowered his instrument. All the television monitors in Churchill Downs were now focused on the University of Louisville Marching Band, which began playing the opening notes of "My Old Kentucky Home."

Oh, the sun shines bright on my...

Cal realized he could do nothing until the song was over, so he gave in to the moment and embraced the emotion coursing through all of Churchill Downs as the band played the most sentimental song in history.

People all around him were singing along with the music. There wasn't a dry eye in the place when the final chorus kicked in and the band ramped up the crescendo.

Weep no more my lady, oh! Weep no more today!
We will sing one song for the Old Kentucky Home,
For My Old Kentucky Home far a-way!

The audience ripped into a wild applause as the song concluded. Hats were thrown into the air and everyone hugged each other and cheered. Even Cal had a tear in his eye as he found himself caught in the emotion of the moment. You never know how powerful that song is until you hear it sung at the Kentucky Derby.

But they had no time to be sentimental. The instant the crowd loosened, Cal and Harper made a break for it. The back of the crowd opened up first, so they gained a few seconds on their one-eyed assailant.

They reached the Millionaires Row private elevator and Harper scanned her pass to unlock it. The door opened. They slipped inside and pressed the button that would take them upstairs.

The button lit up, but the doors hesitated. Through the open doors, they spotted the grey fedora in a full sprint toward them. Their assailant knocked a woman down and continued without stopping. People were yelling angrily at him to stop running, but he seemed not to hear them.

Cal pressed the elevator button repeatedly.

"Close, damnit! Close!"

The man was only a few feet away now. He reached into his coat and slid a small pistol from a hidden holster as he ran.

"Oh no! He has a gun!" Harper shouted and she ducked down in the elevator.

Suddenly the doors began closing. The man extended his arm and pointed the gun directly at Cal.

At the last possible second, the elevator door snapped shut and they were safe.

"Oh my god that was close!" Harper exclaimed. "He had a gun! How did he have a gun in here?!"

Cal couldn't even respond. His shirt was soaked in sweat and he was fighting for air. That was far too close for comfort.

The elevator dinged when it reached the top floor. Cal and Harper stepped off still gasping for breath and trying to regain their composure. They were once again standing in the luxurious and serene Millionaires Row dining room as though nothing had happened.

Evelyn, the woman from their table, was just walking out of the Ladies' Room as Cal and Harper exited the elevator.

"Oh, so glad you're back! We wondered if we would have you up here for the race. I know they have the new owner's box downstairs, but it seems to me we have the best view of the track. My goodness, are you nervous? You both look like you just ran a lap around the track yourselves! Dear me, I do believe you need a drink. Come, dears. We have less than ten minutes!"

Cal and Harper couldn't begin to explain themselves. They allowed Evelyn to lead them to the observation deck where they staked a claim against the railing. From here, they would watch the main event.

34

"Harper, you are looking good at 2 to 1 right now. Valkyrie is still the favorite," Harold said to the group as they stood on the balcony watching the horses circle the starting gates.

"I have never been so nervous for anything in my life," Harper replied. "How much time until post?"

"Eight minutes."

The balcony was buzzing with excitement. Everyone in Millionaires Row was standing on the tiered observation deck watching the track with anticipation. They all knew the owner of the Derby favorite was in their midst, but no one wanted to jinx her by wishing her good luck.

"Mr. Diamond, did you place a bet?" asked the woman who had brought Cal to the table when he first entered Millionaires Row.

"You know, I got caught up in the excitement and forgot to do it. Should I?"

"Of course you should! You are standing next to the winning owner for goodness sake! Hurry in there!"

Might as well, Cal thought. Excusing himself, he reentered the dining room. He walked up to the betting window and took a spot in line.

While he waited, he surveyed the room for any sign of the grey suit. Nothing. He trained his eyes on the elevator door and watched carefully each time it opened just in case it contained the gun-toting goon.

Cal wished he had the plastic weapon Clint Stevens had showed him at the gun shop. He hated being unarmed in the face of an enemy who was packing heat. How were all of these people getting guns in here? Gallo's man had one and so did Joe Brand's guy with the security badge. I thought this place was supposed to be on lockdown?

If the man in the grey suit managed to get up here to Millionaires Row, they would be sitting ducks. Gallo's lackey clearly had no qualms about brandishing a weapon in public. Cal wondered what had happened after the elevator door had closed. Maybe the one-eyed madman was apprehended by security. After all, he did have a handgun fully exposed in the middle of the paddock.

"Sir? Excuse me, sir. How can I help you?"

Cal started when he heard the voice calling him back to reality. It was his turn to bet.

"Oh, yes, sorry. I'd like $100 on the 3 to win, please."

"Yes, sir. You like the favorite then, eh?"

"I do."

Cal handed over a $100-dollar bill and was given a betting ticket in exchange. He examined the ticket as he walked away from the window.

$100 WIN

3 VALKYRIE

"Okay, Valkyrie. Let's see what you've got," he said aloud. Cal took one last look at the Millionaires Row elevator. Still nothing out of the ordinary, so he stepped back out on the balcony and retook his spot next to Harper.

"Imagine," Harper was saying, "if Kyna becomes the first female jockey ever to win the Derby. Wouldn't that be something? And on my horse!"

"It would be a truly historic moment for the sport," said Evelyn. "I have waited for this moment for four decades. This could be our year!"

"Sterling picked her to ride Valkyrie almost a year ago. It was well before our horse had earned enough qualifying points to secure his spot in the race. We just knew he was a special thoroughbred and the connection Kyna has with him is obvious," Harper replied. "They were made for each other."

"TWO MINUTES TO POST! TWO MINUTES TO POST!" boomed the announcer's voice over the loudspeaker.

"Oh my gosh, y'all. I'm about to *die*!" Harper exclaimed.

One of the women hugged Harper and patted her shoulder.

"Here, Frank, have a look at the starting gates," Harold said, handing his binoculars to Cal.

Cal took the binoculars from him. "Are you sure?"

"Yes, yes. I have seen dozens of these, my boy! You are a first timer. By all means, I insist."

Cal raised the binoculars to his eyes and focused them on the starting gates. He could see all twenty horses lined up in a row just a few feet from the green metal structure as they waited to be loaded into the chutes.

The horses were pawing at the ground and their eyes were darting back and forth. Some backed up and a few were even rearing slightly as their jockeys led them forward. The horses sensed the excitement in the air and they too were overcome with nerves.

"The silks are amazing," Cal spoke to no one in particular as he moved the binoculars from one horse to the next.

"Indeed," answered Harold. "The farms all pick their colors and design the jockey's silks themselves. It makes for a beautiful photo."

Then Cal spotted Valkyrie. He was standing stone-still before the starting gate as the other horses fidgeted and pranced around him. He stared stoically forward, immune to the nerves of his fellow thoroughbreds.

Kyna Ryan was patting Valkyrie's neck. Through the binoculars, Cal could see she was leaning forward and calmly whispering into her horse's ear. Kyna's goggles rested on her forehead and her crop was under her left arm. Cal wondered if she would use it during the race.

As he watched Kyna and Valkyrie, another horse suddenly entered his field of view. The new horse was stark white. Ghostly. His lips and nose carried a pinkish hue against the white coat. The jockey riding him wore white silks with light blue stripes and a yellow sun emblazoned on the back. Cal recognized the colors from the Argentine flag. It was Gallo's horse Calavera.

Cal couldn't deny that Gallo's horse looked powerful. He trotted with an air of pride, snorting and jostling the other thoroughbreds near him.

"That four horse sure looks tough," Cal said as he pulled the binoculars away from his face. "How about that glowing white coloration? You don't see that often."

"No you don't," Harold answered. "Some argue a white horse is an indicator of poor genetics. Not too many of them run at this level. But I agree. He looks good for such a longshot. And he comes in with a good record. Of course, so do all of the other horses in this field. The best of the best. Even a 50 to 1 has a shot. Stranger things have happened."

"You think he can win?" Cal asked.

"I certainly would not put it past him. He has a strong lineage and he ran well in the Florida Derby a few weeks ago. Besides, Augusto Gallo is no slouch. He knows horses."

Cal shuddered slightly at the name of his rival. He studied the electronic board in the center of the infield that displayed the odds of each entry. As promised, Gallo had orchestrated a 50-1 line at the post for his horse. He had successfully made Calavera a longshot. Could he pull off the rest of his insane plan?

Cal wondered how many of the horses on the track had been visited by Gallo's veterinarian. How many of them were under the influence of his secret cocktail? In a race like the Derby, all he would need to do is make the horses run two seconds slower than their usual pace. That would be a big enough margin to change the finish. Two fewer heartbeats per minute and the race would be lost.

As he stood on the balcony watching the horses, Cal felt powerless. He had protected Harper's horse, but what of the rest? Had he done enough? Surely Valkyrie could beat Calavera one-on-one in the absence of foul play. Would Gallo tip his hand in frustration?

Cal decided once the race was over and everyone was safe, he would find Gallo and turn up the heat no matter the consequences. He could not let Gallo escape even if his Derby plot was foiled. But then again, what if Calavera wins? Gallo will be paraded around as a hero. Every media outlet in Churchill Downs will want an interview. He might be unstoppable.

Cal raised the binoculars to his eyes and again located Kyna Ryan's red and black silks.

Calavera bumped in close to Valkyrie, and the jockey leaned over and said something to Kyna. She scrunched her face with a look of disgust. Whatever the jockey had said, Kyna didn't like it. She stared forward and ignored the beast and rider to her right.

The portrait of the two horses standing side by side painted a striking contrast. One jet black and the other milky white—almost albino. Their colors were exactly opposite each other and that binary was all the more emphasized by their close proximity.

"Look, they are being loaded!" someone shouted on the balcony next to him.

Cal swung the binoculars left to post position one and saw that, sure enough, the first horse had been loaded into the starting gates. Next went horse number two and the gate slammed shut on its flanks.

Then it was Valkyrie's turn to enter the starting gates. Kyna nudged him forward by squeezing her heels against his belly. He eased into the gate and disappeared from Cal's view.

Calavera went in immediately after Valkyrie. One by one, right down the line, each horse was loaded into the starting gates.

Cal's stomach churned as he watched and waited. They were only seconds away from the post. The volume at Churchill Downs had gone from a deafening roar of excitement and anticipation to an eerie hushed silence once the horses began to take their positions. Everyone knew the main event was moments away. The bets were all placed. The only thing left to do now was wait to see if history would be made.

Through the lenses of the binoculars, Cal watched the 20th horse enter the chute.

"They're in!" he announced to the group.

The entirety of Churchill Downs froze. All the spectators inhaled and held their breath. The stadium was a giant vacuum and the collective gasp from the crowd sucked all the oxygen from the 115-acre property in one flashing instant. It felt as though they were on the surface of the moon, stuck in a vacuum entirely devoid of sound. Churchill Downs was a black hole. The giant inhale took with it all the senses and all the traces of human emotion, and for a split second nothing remained but a floating mirage of twenty horses and twenty jockeys.

The announcer's voice resounded through the deafening silence and echoed throughout the city of Louisville.

"They're at the post!"

Hold. No one breathe. No one move. There is no air. There is no dirt. There are no seats. There is no railing. There are no people.

The starting bell ripped a hole in the stadium. It tore Churchill Downs in half like a giant sheet of paper. RIIIIIIIIIIIIINNNNNGGGG!!!

"AND THEY'RE OFF!!!!"

The gates slammed open and twenty horses broke from the metal structure at full gallop. The stadium erupted with thunderous applause. The race was on!

High above the track, Cal, Harper, and the rest of the crew cheered for the horse they hoped would come out on top.

"Come on 3!"

"Go Valkyrie!"

"Get 'em, Kyna!"

"How did he break? How did he break?" asked Harper excitedly.

"He looks good from here," replied Harold. "He's a nose ahead of the pack, just off the rail. The good news is he's not pinned."

Cal knew with a 20-horse field, a bad break from the post could spell disaster. If a horse couldn't get out in front of the pack, he might get pinned against the rail and hemmed in by the other runners, preventing a break to the outside that would allow him to pass the competition.

The rapid-fire call of the track announcer was singing through the loudspeaker, relaying the running position of the horses. Like an old-time radio host he rattled off the call:

"Coming around the first turn it's the favorite Valkyrie by a nose, followed closely by Maxwell's Cadence on the inside. Holding third is Freeport with Stratford

Seeker running strong in fourth. Fifth place is the longshot from Argentina Calavera and the rest of the pack is right on his heels…"

Cal zoomed the binoculars on Kyna Ryan as the horses hit the back stretch. She was ducked forward and holding hard to the reins on Valkyrie's neck. She gripped the crop in her hand but was not using it yet. The horse was running strong on his own accord. He had the lead by a nose. Each time the horse lunged forward, he edged slightly past the second runner Maxwell's Cadence.

"Kyna's letting him run. They look good!" Cal announced to the balcony with the binoculars still fixed on his eyes.

"I'm so nervous! My heart is pounding in my stomach!"

"And the favorite Valkyrie is holding on to a thin lead coming out of the back stretch. Ladies and gentlemen, they have hit the halfway point in this running of the Kentucky Derby! Freeport and Stratford Seeker are slipping off the pace set by the lead horse—now back a length from the top two contenders. Valkyrie and Maxwell's Cadence look to be pulling away from the pack. But wait! Here comes Calavera grinding up the outside. Folks, he's making a play at the leaders! Will this longshot challenge? He looks to be running strong and gaining ground. Calavera now holds third place!"

"Oh no!" shouted Evelyn. "Where does he think he's going?"

"The longshot is running strong. He's making the other horses look like they are standing still!" another man on the balcony proclaimed.

Cal removed the binoculars from his eyes and glanced quickly at Harper. She returned his look with fear in her eyes as she bit her lower lip. Cal turned back to the track and continued watching.

"We're now a quarter mile out, folks, and it has become a three-horse race! The rest of the pack is falling back as we enter the final turn. And Maxwell's Cadence has now taken the lead for the first time in the race! Calavera is on Valkyrie's flank just a length off the leader! And they are coming up on the final stretch. We have ourselves a horse race! This is going to be a big finish, folks! Get your cameras ready!"

As the horses hit the home stretch, the crowd raised the volume yet another notch. Cal could barely hear anyone around him for the noise in the stadium. Everyone was cheering for their horse to win.

"Come on Valkyrie! You can do it!"

"Ladies and gentlemen, they have hit the home stretch! Here they come! Who will finish on top?!"

Watching through the binoculars, Cal could see all three of the top horses were now within a nose of each other. As they opened up the gallop in the final stretch, they ran with only inches separating one horse from the next. The jockeys were close enough to shake hands.

The riders on Maxwell's Cadence and Calavera had taken out their whips. They were driving their horses with everything in them, whipping their flanks to motivate them onward. Kyna had yet to take a single swat at Valkyrie. He was running completely on his own accord.

"Don't look now folks, but we have a record pace at the third quarter! We could see it happen! Can they do it?!"

"Oh my god!" exhaled Harper to Cal's left.

"Two hundred yards to go! Two hundred yards to go! Maxwell's Cadence looks to be tiring. He's dropping back and the four horse Calavera has overtaken him for the lead by a nose! We have a 50 to 1 longshot leading the pack, folks! Will he pull off the upset of the century?!"

"Come on 3! You can do it!" the balcony was shouting.

"Here we go! One hundred yards remain. This. is. it! It's down to Calavera and Valkyrie now. One will win and one will place! They are neck and neck!"

Calavera's jockey was whipping his horse repeatedly, goading him on. Kyna was doing nothing other than clutching the reins and ducking behind Valkyrie's neck to reduce wind resistance. She was letting Valkyrie do exactly what he was born to do. Dirt was flying all around the stampeding thoroughbreds.

"Do not blink! It's a photo finish!" the announcer shouted as the horses were mere seconds from the finish line.

Suddenly, Valkyrie begin inching forward. Calavera's lead disappeared and the two horses were neck and neck. Cal kept the binoculars focused on their noses. He could see the giant nostrils flaring as the horses gulped oxygen.

"And Valkyrie has taken the lead! Calavera is tiring! It's Valkyrie by a nose and he's still pushing! Valkyrie is really pouring it on now! Where did he find the stamina?! He's pulling ahead! He has taken the lead by nearly a length! This race belongs to Valkyrie! He's racing against himself and the Derby winners who came before him! Look at that horse run, folks!"

The balcony was going crazy all-around Cal. He dropped the binoculars from his eyes and watched as

Valkyrie blew across the finish line at a blistering gallop. He had Calavera by a full length. The cheering crowd thundered through the stadium and shook the balcony where they stood.

"Ladies and gentlemen, look at the board! Look! He has done it! A new Derby record! Valkyrie has broken Secretariat's speed record! One minute fifty-nine seconds flat! He's done it! A new record! History has been made! What a race!"

"Fantastic!" exclaimed Harold to Cal's right. "Magnificent performance."

"Harper, she did it! Kyna did it!" congratulated Evelyn.

Harper was in shock. She was speechless and awestruck. She was laughing and crying at the same time. Cal patted her shoulder and congratulated her.

Evelyn and the other ladies immediately went into action and ushered Harper off the balcony. They were fixing her hair and touching up her makeup.

"Get ready for the media storm, honey. You are about to be swamped," one of the women was saying as she dabbed at Harper's eyes. "We need to get you down to the Winner's Circle ASAP."

Harper still hadn't spoken a word. She seemed unable to find any utterance befitting the moment. She stopped at the balcony door and turned back to Cal and the men on the observation deck. She looked right into Cal's eyes.

"Thank you. Thank you so much. I know Sterling thanks you, too."

Cal felt a knot in his throat and feared he might choke up if he spoke, so he just nodded and stared back into her eyes.

Then she was gone, whisked away by the group of women. Cal watched through the glass as they hit the elevator and headed downstairs.

Suddenly, Cal remembered what he was doing. The elevator! Gallo! What will he do? He knew Harper would be safe in the watchful eyes of the media for now, but once the cameras were gone what would happen?

"What's wrong, old boy? This is a time for celebration. You look like you've seen a ghost," Harold said once Harper and the women were gone.

Cal turned to Harold and handed him back the binoculars.

"Thanks for these," he said. "There will be no ghosts today. Not if I can help it."

Cal left Harold standing on the balcony alone, holding his binoculars with a puzzled look on his face.

35

As soon as Cal's feet hit the paddock ground, he began searching the crowd for Gallo and his men. Most owners would be happy with a second-place finish in the Derby, but Cal knew it would not be good enough for Gallo. After all his plan was to win, so nothing less would suffice. The defeat would have him furious—especially considering it came at the hand of the rival he had murdered in order to orchestrate his grand scheme.

Cal tried to make his way trackside where he knew Harper would be in the Winner's Circle with her horse, but tens of thousands of spectators were now moving in the opposite direction. As soon as the featured race ended, the stands had cleared out. Everyone was hoping to beat the traffic jam that would soon paralyze the streets around Churchill Downs.

Fighting the current of the crowd was a losing battle, like trying to walk through a brick wall. Cal was making no progress. The throngs of people might as well have been sewn together. Every step Cal gained was followed by two steps backward. Forward movement was impossible in the face of the impenetrable crowd.

A huge television monitor was mounted atop the paddock entry. Cal pressed himself against the cement wall and looked up at the television while the swarming mass elbowed past him.

On the screen, he could see Harper standing next to Valkyrie and Kyna. The winning thoroughbred was draped with the customary coat of roses that adorns every Derby winner.

Cameras flashed all around Harper as reporters asked her questions. Cal couldn't hear her responses. He watched as she smiled and indicated toward the horse and jockey behind her.

He hated not being near her in case Gallo tried something, but there was no possible way he could fight the crushing crowd. All he could do was watch the monitor and stand helplessly against the wall as thousands of people jostled past him.

Where was Gallo? How could Cal possibly find him in this melee? Cal had not anticipated the sheer volume and force of the mass exodus from Churchill Downs. All of his plans were rendered inconsequential in the face of the crowd.

Cal's only hope was that Gallo's frustration and cockiness would get the better of him and cause him to eventually blow his own cover. For now, he would have to wait.

He stopped at a betting window on his way out of the track to cash his winning ticket.

"Hey, that's a nice payday!" said the man behind the counter cheerily. He wore a green visor that cast a neon pall over his face. The man counted out $300 and handed it over to Cal.

Cal tapped the bills on the counter to collect them and placed them in his pocket. All around him people were bumping and pushing as the paddock area swelled beyond capacity.

Once outside, Cal made a beeline for the MG where his .38 was stashed. As he walked, he checked his phone for missed calls or texts from Harper. Nothing. The airwaves were jammed up. No calls could go in or out with the cell towers this saturated.

The streets around Churchill Downs looked like Mardi Gras. People were everywhere. They were drinking, slurring, shouting, swaying as they headed to their cars. Trash littered the sidewalks and yards in the Derby aftermath.

Traffic on Central Avenue was more congested than a red ant colony. Cal knew he was in for a long wait, so he fell in line and got comfortable.

He scanned the packed streets for a recognizable face. Harper and the owners probably had some kind of secret exit out the back of Churchill Downs. For all Cal knew, they had a helicopter pad in the stables for easy access.

Cal tapped his fingers on the steering wheel as he waited. The top was down on his convertible and the evening sun was sinking over Churchill Downs. He scanned the radio for any reports of foul play, any signs of a Gallo attack.

Soon his thoughts drifted to the woman he had spent the past two months with. What had gone wrong? Just when he was starting to feel something for Emma, she had pushed him away. He was even entertaining thoughts of a future with her, but that was all gone now. Her square-jawed companion had taken Cal's place and closed the book on their budding romance.

I should have known, Cal thought. Emma is out of my league. She grew up attending expensive private schools with wealthy parents who own box seats at the Kentucky Derby. How could I ever think she would seriously consider a guy like me? It never would have worked. Probably for the better to end things now. Besides, I put her through hell last week. She would be crazy *not* to move on after the week we had.

All of these thoughts were rolling around in Cal's head. He was doing his best to justify her sudden change of heart. Trying hard to convince himself he would be better off without Emma in his life. But deep down inside, her romantic spurning hurt him.

He drove on in silence, searching the sidewalks for one last glimpse of her.

Eventually, the traffic loosened up and Churchill Downs grew smaller and smaller in Cal's rear view. He raised the top on the MG prior to hitting the interstate. Before he knew it, his Derby day adventure was over, and he was headed back to Lexington.

That night, Cal wrestled with the question of what to do next. The excitement of the past month had culminated that afternoon at Churchill Downs. Harper Halcott's horse had won the Derby and set a new speed record. They had all made it through race day without any incident.

Cal sat on his back porch and stared into the yard. Dusk was approaching. Fireflies began to flicker. Like tiny lighthouses, they announced approaching danger with each pulse of light. Turn back or you will be dashed against the rocks, they seemed to say. Cal wanted to heed their warning, but he wasn't sure how. He sat quietly in his chair and sipped from a glass of bourbon.

The problem of Augusto Gallo remained. Gallo had confessed to the murder of Sterling Halcott, but Cal still had no proof of the crime other than his own testimony. If Gallo had done something stupid in public, they could have put him away. Until Cal had more evidence or unless Gallo betrays his guilt, there wasn't much that could be done. More than likely, Gallo was already on a plane back to Argentina where he would lick his wounds and prepare for another strike.

And that was the biggest remaining problem. Gallo had attempted to have Cal killed at least twice. Why would he stop now? Would Cal be forced to live the rest of his life in fear of Gallo's next attack? That would be no way to live.

The light faded from the horizon. Cal's back porch gradually became shrouded in darkness as he sipped the bourbon and pondered his next move. He didn't budge from his patio chair for several hours except to occasionally refill the rocks glass sitting on the table next to him.

As the night wore on, he became more and more drunk. Emma was gone and the hope of anything good coming from that relationship had vanished. One more disappointment in a long line of disappointments. On the other hand, Harper was safe. Maybe Gallo would just disappear. But Cal had promised Harper he would clear Sterling's name. Anyway, he couldn't just let a killer go free. Something must be done.

Somewhere around 3:00 a.m. Cal's fingertips slipped from the rocks glass and dropped peacefully to his lap. His head nodded forward and his body slouched in the vinyl patio chair. Tomorrow is another day and his questions would be waiting when he awoke. For tonight, Cal surrendered his restless mind to the darkness that enveloped him.

36

BUZZZZZZZZZZ.
BUZZZZZZZZZZ.
BUZZZZZZZZZZ.

Cal shot up in his chair and searched for the source of the loud noise.

"What the?" he grumbled. "Where the heck?"

He suddenly realized he was in his backyard in the exact place he had fallen asleep a few hours before. Daylight was just breaking, and he could barely make out the shapes of trees in his yard as his eyes adjusted to the dim light of dawn.

The buzzing sound was coming from his cell phone on the glass table to his right. He glanced at his watch. 6:15 a.m.

"Who the hell is calling me?"

He grabbed the phone and examined the caller ID.

"Oh no, it's Harper!"

Suddenly, Cal came to his senses. He fought the hangover pounding through his body. Shaking his head to clear the cobwebs, he put the phone to his ear. With a groggy voice, he answered the call.

"Harper? What is it? Are you okay?"

The voice that answered did not belong to Harper.

"Good morning, Mr. Tyson. Sounds as though you had a, how do you say, *tortured* night. Funny coincidence because your red-headed friend had a bit of a *tortured* night of her own."

The Spanish accent changed abruptly to a ringing, maniacal laughter.

"Gallo! What have you done? Where are you?"

"You and the widow bitch have fucked up everything. I told you not to mess with me, but you couldn't mind your own business. It is time to end this once and for all."

"Tell me where you are."

Cal heard Gallo's voice move away from the phone. He was talking to someone else in the room.

"Tell your boyfriend where we are."

"Cal! Help! He's crazy! Please hurry!"

Harper was frantic. Her voice was strained as she pleaded through her tears.

Gallo silenced her and returned the receiver to his own mouth.

"You have until sunrise to join us at the Halcott Mansion. If you come, I will consider letting her live. If you are late, or if you try anything funny, I promise I will kill you both," Gallo snarled into the phone. "Don't be late. The clock is ticking."

The phone went dead in Cal's hand.

Cal jumped up from his seat and tried to gather himself. Immediately, his legs wobbled, and he dropped back into the chair. He placed his hands on the table and raised himself again, this time pausing to steady himself. He had drunk enough last night to take down a horse. The liquor was still in his blood. It clouded his brain and confused his limbs as he tried to move them. His legs refused to work the way he wanted them to, and his eyes weren't focusing properly.

"Nothing like fighting a mad man to the death at dawn...while drunk."

He stumbled inside and threw some water on his face in a desperate attempt to sober up. He grabbed the .38 which was still on the counter from last night. Streaks of dawn cracked the skyline when Cal pulled open his front door. The MG fired up, and he was on his way to Woodford County.

The roads were empty at dawn on Sunday morning. The entire state of Kentucky had a hangover, and everyone was still in bed sleeping it off. As Cal sped west toward the Halcott Estate, the sunrise chased him in the rearview mirror.

He wished he was still in bed with the rest of the state. The adrenaline of the moment was distracting his mind from the alcohol's influence, but there was no denying he was a far cry from clear-headed.

Cal dialed Joe Brand's number when he hit the county line.

"Good morning, sunshine. Did you finally decide to join my Sunday morning racquetball game?" Joe asked when he answered the phone.

"Joe, the shit is hitting the fan. I need backup at the Halcott Estate."

Joe's demeanor immediately changed when he heard Cal's tone.

"Is it Gallo? Do you have him? What's going on?"

"Everything was relatively quiet at the race yesterday, thanks to your security detail. But Gallo's gone mad. He has snapped and he's holding Harper hostage. It sounds bad—like they have been at it all night."

"Then time is of the essence. I'll make some calls and get a S.W.A.T. team out there stat."

"No. We need to keep it quiet. He threatened her life if the police show up. I'm going in alone first. But if you can have some guys gather on the edge of the property and wait, that would be perfect. This is our chance to put him away for good."

"Cal, don't try to be a hero here. We have a special ops team trained for these scenarios."

"I need you to trust me, Joe. This is why I'm talking to you and not a 911 operator. This situation calls for finesse and discretion."

"We will be there as quickly as possible. Don't do anything stupid, man. Be careful."

"Roger that. Thanks."

By the time Cal hung up, he was approaching the welded iron gates that marked the entry of the Halcott driveway. The top of the sun was just cracking the horizon behind him and the grounds of the estate were illuminated by a pinkish hue. A thin fog blanketed the field and hovered over the pond at the front of the property. The bluegrass glistened with fresh dew.

One of the black iron gates hung sideways on its hinges. The twisted metal was mangled and scratched. It had been forced open and the huge gate now swung loosely back and forth in the morning breeze.

Cal eased the car between the open gates. As he did, he spotted the security camera mounted on the stone wall to his left. Was he being watched?

He drove the familiar driveway he had traveled only a few weeks earlier. Between the two ponds and through the long stretch of pines. As before, the morning sunlight disappeared when he entered the thick undergrowth. Cal kept his eyes peeled for traps. His car was an easy target for ambush in this dense forest. The .38 sat in his lap with the safety switched off.

Around every bend in the driveway Cal assumed a posse would be waiting to open fire on him, but he somehow passed through the pines without incident. Just before the forest ended, Cal killed the engine of the MG and coasted off the road. He parked the car behind a group of trees and got out. He slowly crept to the edge of the woods and surveyed the scene in front of him.

The sun was climbing over the field to the east. The front facade of the Halcott Mansion faced the sunrise. It was glowing with the morning light.

Cal immediately spotted the intruders' cars parked haphazardly around the Halcotts' circle driveway and fountain. Gallo and his men had taken over the plantation. He counted four cars. That could easily mean 10 men or more. No way he could take them all. Cal wondered if Brand had arrived yet with backup. He pressed himself against the tree and watched carefully for any sign of life.

The front of the property was silent. No movement. No sound other than the low idle of the vehicles in the driveway. Cal was close enough to smell the exhaust fumes wafting from the tailpipes.

After a few minutes of surveillance, Cal was satisfied he could make a move. He stepped out from behind the tree and made a break for the nearest car. When he reached it, he threw himself against the side and again shielded his body from view.

Still nothing. His presence had not been spotted.

He made three more jumps like this one, and within a few minutes he had maneuvered his way to the side of the house. He leaned against the mansion, breathing heavily, with his pistol raised.

For the first time, he could hear sounds of life. Voices. They were coming from around back. He remembered from his first visit that behind the house was a garden, and he guessed this was the site of the gathering.

He listened quietly. The voices were too faint to make out.

Cal peeked around the side of the house. There was a guard only a few feet away, but his back was to the front of the mansion. Good thing, too, because he and Cal would have been face to face if the guard were doing his job properly.

The guard carried an AK-47 attached to a strap slung over his shoulder. At the moment, the weapon hung loosely at his side while he lit a cigarette. He had turned to shield the wind from his flaming match. He was ducked against the side of the house with his hand cupped around the white cigarette. The pungent odor of burning phosphorous filled Cal's nostrils as he slipped around the corner.

Cal wasted no time. He silently covered the short distance and grabbed the guard from behind. The guard struggled and reached for his weapon, but Cal gave his head a sharp twist. The man went limp and dropped to the grass at Cal's feet.

"Haven't you heard smoking kills?" Cal muttered as he advanced past the man and continued toward the back of the mansion.

He kept his eyes peeled for another sentinel. The coast was clear, so he resumed his approach with the .38 raised in front of him.

By the time he reached the back corner of the mansion, he could hear everything. The voices were only a few feet away, but his view was obscured by the 8-foot shrubs that surrounded the garden.

"A shame to wreck such a pretty face," Gallo was saying. "But the sun is almost up, and it looks like your knight in shining armor has forsaken you."

Cal leaned quietly forward and found a tiny hole in the bushes through which he could see the garden. Gallo was pacing back and forth in front of Harper's chair. Her head was lolling forward and her arms were tied behind her back. One of Gallo's goons stood on either side of the chair, and both men were armed. The garden appeared to be empty otherwise.

"Your husband was a chump. And now your boyfriend is a chump, too. Perhaps you should try picking better men," Gallo continued.

Harper raised her head and stared at Gallo. "Screw you."

The men laughed at her futile epithet.

"Hmm…yes…not a bad idea perhaps," Gallo replied. "I can think of a few ways we can spend your final minutes alive…"

As he spoke, he ran the barrel of his pistol down the side of her cheek. She shuddered and pulled her head away from his hand.

"I would rather die right now."

"In that case, I would hate to disappoint you," Gallo said. He withdrew the pistol from her cheek. He cocked it and pointed it directly at her head.

"One meddling Halcott down, one to go."

Cal knew he needed to act fast. He had to do something, or else Harper would be killed right before his eyes. He spotted a break in the shrub wall surrounding the garden and charged through with his .38 leveled at the group of men.

"Hold it right there, Gallo, or I'll blow a hole through you."

Gallo slowly lowered his weapon.

"So nice of you to finally join us. You are just in time to watch the sunrise. Care for a mimosa, Mr. Tyson? They go well with Derby hangovers," Gallo said sarcastically.

His voice and facial expression were calm despite the gun aimed at him. It was as though he dealt with loaded weapons every day.

"Drop the gun and raise your hands slowly," Cal said.

"Oh, but where is the fun in that? Should we not have a shoot-out? I know you Kentuckians love your duels."

"Cut the crap and toss your weapon. And tell one of your goons to untie her."

Gallo slowly laid his weapon on the ground in front of him.

"Them too. Untie her," Cal directed. "Or I promise you won't walk out of this garden."

Gallo nodded at his men and they also dropped their guns and started to untie Harper's hands.

"Might I ask what your plan is, Mr. Tyson? My men will never let you leave these grounds alive."

"We'll see about that," Cal replied. "The better question is what *your* plan is. Did you think you would get away with this half-brained scheme?"

"Patience, Mr. Tyson. My plans will be revealed in due time."

"Wrong answer. Your time is running out."

"Just the opposite I'm afraid!" Gallo announced and began laughing maniacally.

"Cal, watch out!" Harper shouted.

But it was too late. Cal felt the cold metal of a pistol press against the side of his head. One of Gallo's other men had snuck up behind him.

"Now it is your turn to drop the weapon. I told you this would not end well for you. And your insolence has brought death for both you and the girl! Now do as I say and put down your gun!"

Cal knew if he surrendered, he and Harper would both be dead in a matter of seconds. He had nothing to lose. Might as well take a chance.

He began to slowly bend over and place the gun on the dew-covered grass. As he did, the man next to him slightly relaxed his own weapon. That was the window of opportunity Cal needed.

He quickly swung his arm to the right and swept at the gunman's legs. The man's feet slid easily on the wet grass and, with one swipe, he was on the ground. Cal rolled left and discharged a bullet into his fallen adversary before the assailant could recover.

Immediately popping up on one knee, Cal fired two shots at Gallo's goons on either side of Harper. The .38 was as trusty as ever. Both shots found their mark and the men dropped with a thud.

Harper ducked and covered her head in terror. Her arms were freed.

"Run!" Cal shouted at her.

She wasted no time in heeding his advice. She hopped up from the chair and took off for the back of the garden. Cal followed right on her heels.

Behind them they could hear Gallo shouting as he fumbled for his gun on the ground.

"Guards! Guards! Don't let them get away!"

Gallo recovered his pistol and squeezed off two rounds in Cal's and Harper's direction, but they had already rounded the corner of the shrub and disappeared out of sight.

Cal and Harper passed through the opening in the bushes and they were immediately confronted with a second wall of shrubbery. They turned right only to find another wall awaiting them.

"Where the heck are we?" Cal asked, gasping for air.

"The garden maze!" Harper answered. She too was struggling to catch her breath.

Cal looked at her and realized for the first time Harper's face was badly beaten and bruised. Gallo had really done a number on her. He wanted to ask her about it, but there was no time now.

"Can you get us out of here?"

"I, I don't know. It has been so long since I've tried it. John Hood is the maze expert."

Cal flashed back to his conversation with Hood when he had first toured the Halcott estate. He remembered John saying no guest had ever solved the maze.

"Try hard. Our lives depend on it!"

The two sprinted down the green corridor with Gallo and his men hot on their trail.

37

Cal and Harper ran deeper and deeper into the garden maze. Each turn led to another wall of tall, impenetrable bushes. John Hood wasn't kidding about the maze's difficulty. Time and again they hit dead ends and were forced to retrace their steps. Their only hope was Gallo's men were also foiled by the maze's twists and turns.

As they ran, they could hear their pursuers close behind shouting angrily in Spanish. Their footsteps fell heavily on the grassy path.

Occasional gunshots echoed through the maze and bullets whizzed in the air. Each time the men got too close, Cal paused for a moment and squeezed a few rounds back at them to slow their progress.

"¡El otro lado!" one of the men shouted.

"Oh no," Cal said under his breath.

"What is it?" Harper asked.

"The other side," Cal replied. "They are trying to flank us."

"But if they come from both sides, we'll be trapped in the middle!"

Cal knew she was right. He hoped they would beat the welcoming party to the other side.

Just then, they rounded a corner and hit the center of the maze. The garden walls opened to an expansive network of flower beds and walking paths interspersed with marble statues. A 15-foot water fountain of carved stone spewed water into a reflecting pool below it. The fountain was the centerpiece of the garden in which they now stood. They were in the eye of the tornado. The halfway point.

The two were pouring sweat and fighting for air.

"This way," Harper whispered.

She took off around a corner and led Cal to a small toolshed that was tucked away behind a wall of bushes. No one would ever spot the shed if they didn't know it was there. It was well-hidden, but still provided a good view of the maze's center.

"We will never make it in the middle of one of these corridors if we get trapped on both sides," Cal breathed. "Our only hope is to hole up here where we have some cover."

Harper nodded. "Didn't you bring anyone out here with you? Are we all alone?"

"Backup is on the way. If we can just hold out until it comes…"

Cal took a position against the side of the shed and peered around the corner. He had a perfect view of both sides of the courtyard. He swept his eyes back and forth between the two maze openings.

The sun was almost completely above the horizon now, but the light was obscured by the tall hedges. The morning shadows stretched long across the courtyard. The warmth of daylight had not yet burned the low mist from the garden's protected inner sanctum.

Cal and Harper watched and waited.

After a few minutes, Gallo appeared in the courtyard with two men. They stepped through the hedge's opening cautiously. Cal watched as Gallo signaled to his men to cross the courtyard while he himself strolled to its center by the trickling fountain. Gallo stood in the middle of the courtyard and slowly turned in a circle, surveying the grounds.

"You are trapped, Mr. Tyson! There is no escape!" he shouted into the emptiness of the courtyard. "Do not prolong the inevitable!"

Gallo's voice echoed throughout the garden. It seemed to come from every direction at once as it reverberated around the empty courtyard and bounced off the marble statues.

"You think you can escape me? You can never escape me!" Gallo continued. "I have eyes everywhere! I saw you with the blonde in downtown Lexington. And again at Cherokee Park in Louisville. I saw you the first time you visited the Halcott Estate. I heard your questions. I had you followed. Remember the BMW? You may have narrowly escaped then, but not today. I have eyes everywhere!"

Cal remembered the black BMW that had chased him away from the mansion the first time he visited. His mind flashed to the narrow bridge and the fiery crash in his rearview mirror. Gallo had been on to him since the beginning. How many of Gallo's men were spies on the farm? Was John Hood one of them? Probably. Cal had a bad feeling about Hood right from the start. And now he was going to die in the maze Hood had designed.

Gallo's threats resounded through the garden as he slowly paced around the base of the fountain. His two guards had reached the other side of the courtyard. They paused and looked back at him, waiting for his orders. Gallo raised a hand and signaled for them to reenter the maze.

Cal turned and looked back at Harper. Her red hair hung loosely on her shoulders. Her right eye was badly swollen, and her face was covered with cuts and bruises. She was exhausted, but her eyes carried a look of determination that pushed Cal to hang on.

They were alone in the courtyard with Gallo now. If they could take him out, they might be able to retrace their steps and make it back out the front of the maze. Of course, the sound of a gunshot would put his goons on high alert. They would immediately circle back and investigate. It might be too risky. For now, their best bet was to wait. Let Gallo shout himself silly while his men search the maze in vain. Surely Brand wasn't far off.

"Did you forget I have already killed one man who got in my way?!" Gallo continued shouting into the courtyard as he paced around the fountain. "Your lives mean nothing to me! You ruined my plans. Everything was perfect. We spent months developing the drug cocktail for the horses. And the bribes! So many greedy pricks! We paid them all!"

Gallo cursed and shook his fist in the air.

"And you think I will let one meddling dick stop me? When I catch you, you will wish you had never heard the name Augusto Gallo!"

Just then, Cal heard the snap of a twig behind him. He and Harper both wheeled around to see the source of the noise. What they saw froze them in their tracks.

The grey suit. The fedora. The eyepatch. The gun leveled right at them.

They had been ambushed from behind!

The man in the grey suit advanced steadily toward them with his weapon raised.

"So we finally meet face to face, Tyson. I have been looking forward to this moment for a long time," the one-eyed man said as he approached. "Let's not waste another minute."

He cocked the handgun and placed his finger on the trigger. Cal and Harper crouched and covered their faces as though it might somehow protect them from the speeding bullets about to penetrate them.

BANG!

BANG!

Silence.

The smoke cleared.

Cal opened his eyes. He felt his chest and head for the entry wound but came up empty. He was unscathed.

The man in the grey suit was lying motionless on the ground in front of them. The back of his grey jacket was soaked in blood.

Behind him stood John Hood. In his hands was a pump-action shotgun. Smoke wafted from the barrel as he hovered over his victim stoically, watching to see if the man made any movement.

"John!" Harper exclaimed. She ran to him and put her arms around his neck. "You saved us!"

Hood pumped his shotgun and stared straight ahead. His eyes surveyed the courtyard for more attackers.

"They may have gotten Mr. Halcott, but they won't get you," Hood spoke gruffly as he secured the area.

By now, Cal had recovered from his shock and he, too, was sweeping the courtyard with his .38. He clearly owed Hood an apology for his misjudgment.

Within seconds, four of Gallo's men came bounding into the opening from the back of the maze. They each took positions of cover behind statues and prepared for the ensuing shootout.

"Kill them all! ¡Ahora!" Gallo shouted. He ducked behind the fountain and waited for the shooting to begin.

But there was no shootout. The swirling blade of a helicopter pierced the morning air. Louder and louder the sound of the rotating engine grew, and within seconds the police chopper was hovering over the green hedges. Moments later, armed police officers in S.W.A.T. gear swarmed the courtyard from the opposite entrance. A loud captain with a bullhorn shouted orders in Spanish from the hovering chopper.

"¡Se rinda! Surrender now! You are surrounded!"

The men tossed their weapons and laid down on the wet grass. Within no time, the police had locked down the area and apprehended Gallo and his men.

Cal and John Hood both tossed their weapons to the ground and waited for the police to reach them. Cal stayed with Harper, while Hood went with the officers to give a statement and debrief.

Once the excitement had subsided and the men were in custody, Cal saw Joe Brand round the corner of the hedgerow and enter the courtyard. Cal waved him down and Brand waded through the path strewn with arresting officers and prostrate bad guys.

"Did you miss that part of the conversation when I said to keep things low key?" Cal asked.

"Hey, it looks to me like you were pretty outnumbered. You better be grateful for the help," Brand retorted. "Besides, the last time I checked, corpses can't play racquetball, so I had no choice."

They shared a strained laugh.

"Well, I should have known you couldn't resist a bust like this one."

"I might be retired, but I wouldn't miss out on all the fun. You know you really need to start giving more respect to the guys in blue. They're not as bad as you think. And they will save your ass now and then if you'll let 'em."

"I guess you're right," Cal replied.

"Ms. Halcott, you have been through a lot these past few months. Are you okay?" asked Brand.

An officer standing nearby handed Harper a blanket and she draped it around her shoulders as she responded to Brand's question.

"Don't worry about me, honey. I'm just fine. In case you missed it, my horse ran the fastest Derby ever yesterday."

"She's still got it," Cal said. He smiled at Harper and winked at Joe Brand.

The three stood silently for a few moments and watched the sunrise paint the rolling fields of Halcott Farms.

Brand nodded in the direction of Gallo, who was being handcuffed about twenty feet away.

"No need to worry about him anymore. He's going away for a long time."

"Yeah? You think the charges will stick?" Cal asked.

"Oh, we heard everything. He shouted his entire confession to anyone who wanted to listen. We were making our way through the maze and caught every word. He led us right to you. Gallo has committed enough crimes to earn a lifetime supply of prison food."

"Thank god," said Harper. "That man has been tormenting our family for years. I can't get rid of him soon enough."

"He won't bother you again," assured Brand.

"What about Sterling? I want to make it clear he had no involvement in this awful plan to hurt the horses and tarnish the Kentucky Derby. Sterling had his faults, but he was a good man and he cared about the horses and the people who work with them."

"Ma'am, the way I understand it, Mr. Halcott died because he refused to go along with Gallo's evil plan. He took a stand for what is right even though it meant putting himself in danger. In my book, we call that a hero," answered Brand with passion in his voice.

Harper nodded. Her eyes welled up.

After a few seconds, Cal spoke out.

"I don't know about you all, but I sure could use a drink."

"Cal, it's not even 8:00 a.m."

"Cut me some slack. It's been a hell of a morning," he answered. "You know what I have heard goes great with a Derby hangover?"

"Mimosas!" Harper exclaimed.

The three laughed and made their way back to the mansion where they did in fact share a round of mimosas on the patio. As the morning sun climbed high over the Bluegrass State, the three toasted to a case closed and to Harper's success at yet another exciting Kentucky Derby.

About the Author

Josh Boldt lives in Lexington, Kentucky with his dog. He is a fan of the thoroughbred industry, and he is no stranger to the local racetracks featured in *The False Favorite*. The next novel in the series is currently underway. Visit joshboldt.com for news and updates.

Made in the USA
Monee, IL
15 June 2020